Old Country Life

S. Baring-Gould

Old Country Life

ISBN: 978-1-64799-604-8

CONTENTS

CHAPTER I

OLD COUNTY FAMILIES

I WONDER whether the day will ever dawn on England when our country houses will be as deserted as are those in France and Germany? If so, that will be a sad day for England. I judge from Germany. There, after the Thirty Years' War, the nobles and gentry set-to to build themselves mansions in place of the castles that had been burnt or battered down. In them they lived till the great convulsion that shook Europe and upset existing conditions social as well as political. Napoleon overran Germany, and the nobles and gentry had not recovered their losses during that terrible period before the State took advantage of their condition to transfer the land to the peasantry. This was not done everywhere, but it was so to a large extent in the south. Money was advanced to the farmers to buy out their landlords, and the impoverished nobility were in most cases glad to sell. They disposed of the bulk of their land, retaining in some cases the ancestral nest, and that only. No doubt that the results were good in one way—but where is a good unmixed? The qualifying evil is considerable in this case.

The gentry or nobility—the terms are the same on the Continent—went to live in the towns. They could no longer afford to inhabit their country mansions. They acquired a taste for town life, its conveniences, its distractions, its amusements; they ceased to feel interest in country pursuits; they only visited their mansions for about eight weeks in the year, for the Sommer-frische. Those who could not afford to furnish two houses, carted that amount of furniture which was absolutely necessary to their country houses for the holiday, and that concluded, carted it back to town again. This state of things continues. Whilst the family is in residence at the Schloss it lives economically; it is there for a little holiday; it does not concern itself with the peasants, the sick, the suffering, the necessitous. It is there—pour s'amuser. The consequence is that the Schloss is without a civilizing influence, without moral force in the place. The country folk have little interest in the family, and the family concerns itself less with the people.

Not only so, but it brings little money into the place. It employs no labour. It is there not to keep open house, but to shut up the purse. In former days the landlord exacted his rents, but then he lived in the midst of his tenants, and the money that came in as rent

1

went out as wage, and in payment for butter, eggs, meat, oats, and hay. The money collected out of a place returned to it again. It is so in many country places in England now where squire and parson live on the land.

In Germany the peasant has stepped out of obligation to the landlord into bondage to the Jew, who receives, but spends nothing. In France the condition is much the same; the great house is a ruin, and so, very generally, is the family that occupies and owns it, if it still lingers on in it.

I remember a stately château of the time of Louis XIV., tenanted by two charming old ladies of the ancienne noblesse, with grand historic names—the last leaves that fluttered on a great family tree, with roots in the remote past; and they fluttered sere to their fall. They walked out every evening in the park attended by their factotum, an old serving-man, who was butler, coachman, gardener, and major-domo. They kept but one female servant, who was cook, lady's-maid, laundress, and house-maid. The old ladies are dead now, and the roof of the château has fallen in. They had no money to spend on the house or in the village, and never was there a village that more needed the circulation in it of a little coin.

Great houses, with us, are only tenanted by their owners when the London season is over; but that is for a good deal longer than the German Sommer-frische; and when the family does come down, it is as rain on a fleece of wool and as the drops that water the earth. It fills the house with guests, and consumes nearly all the market produce of the parish; and at that season, as the people of the place know, money begins to circulate.

It is not, however, my intention to speak of the great mansions of the nobility, but of those of the squirearchy, who are in residence on their estates all the year round.

These houses are elements of considerable blessing to the country. The families of the squires are always in the midst of the people, know the history, and wants, and infirmities of every one. They care for the good of the district. The ladies look after the girls; the squire attends to the condition of the roads and bridges; money is freely spent in the district, and a considerable amount of culture and moral restraint is acquired by those in the classes below, in the farm-houses and the cottages. Such only who have been in parishes that have been for generations squireless, and also in those where a resident family has been planted for centuries, can appreciate the difference in general tone among the people.

Should the time come when the county family will be taken away, then the parish will feel for some time like a mouth from which a molar has been drawn—there will be a vacancy that will cause unrest and discomfort. The molar does not grind and champ to sustain itself alone, but the entire body to which it belongs, and it is much the same with the country squire.

In the sixteenth and seventeenth centuries there were far more resident gentry in the country than there are at present. The number began to dwindle in the eighteenth century. The registers of parishes are instructive in this respect. In a parish there may have been but a single manor, nevertheless there were in it some three or four gentle families, of as good blood as the lord of the manor, inhabiting bartons. Let us take a parish or two as examples. Ugborough in South Devon has valuable registers dating from 1538. In the sixteenth century we find in them the names of the following families, all of gentle blood, occupying good houses—the Spealts, the Prideaux, the Stures, the Fowels, the Drakes, the Glass family, the Wolcombes, the Fountaynes, the Heles, the Crokers, the Percivals. In the seventeenth century occur the Edgcumbes, the Spoores, the Stures, the Glass family again, the Hillerdons, Crokers, Coolings, Heles, Collings, Kempthornes, the Fowells, Williams, Strodes, Fords, Prideaux, Stures, Furlongs, Reynolds, Hurrells, Fownes, Copplestons, and Saverys. In the eighteenth century there are only the Saverys and Prideaux; by the middle of the nineteenth these are gone. The grand old mansion of the Fowells that passed to the Savery family is in Chancery, deserted save by a caretaker, falling to ruins. What other mansions there were in the place are now farm-houses.

Let us take another parish—Staverton. That had in it the grand mansion, Barkington, of the Rowes, who owned other estates in the same parish, in which were settled junior branches of the same family. All have vanished, root and branch. The Woolstones had a noble estate there. They are represented now by a clergyman in the neighbourhood. The Prestons were estated there also; they are gone, and their place knoweth them no more. My own family had two good houses there, Coombe and Pridhamsleigh, from the beginning of the sixteenth century. Both were sold at the end of last century. The Worths of Worth had estates and a house there, and have only a fine monument in the church to testify that they ever lived and died there. In another book I have mentioned the instance of Bratton-Clovelly, where were the Coryndons, Burnabys, Ellacots of Ellacot, Langfords of Langford, Calmadys, Willoughbys, Incledons—all gone, and not one of their houses remaining intact.

The country gentry in those days were not very wealthy. They lived very much on the produce of the home farm, and their younger sons went into trade, and their daughters, without any sense of degradation, married yeomen.

In South Devon, at Slapton, lived in state the Amerideths, deriving from Welsh princes. Griffith Amerideth was the first to settle in Devon; he was a tailor and draper in Exeter, and died in 1559. He married a daughter of a very good family, and his son married the eldest daughter of Lewis Fortescue, one of the Barons of the Exchequer, and his grandchildren married into the Fortescue, Rolle and Loveys families, all of greatest position and fortune in the West.

It has been claimed for the Glanvilles that they are of Norman extraction; they, however, became tanners at Whitchurch, where their tan-pits remain to this day, though their mansion has lost all trace of antiquity. Chief Justice Glanville, who came from this house, and died in 1600, gave it splendour, yet his brother and nephew were not ashamed of the tan-pits, and even allowed a daughter of the house to marry a Tavistock blacksmith, and entered him as "faber" in the pedigree they enrolled with the heralds. The Courtenays of Molland married their daughters to farmers in the place. When, a few years ago, the late Earl of Devon visited Molland, he met a hale old yeoman there named Moggridge. He held out his hand to him; "Cousin," said he, "jump into the carriage with me, and let us have a drive together; we have not met for one hundred and eighty years." When the Woolstones of Staverton registered their pedigree, they considered that there was nothing to be ashamed of to enter one daughter as married to a "clothier," another to an "agricola"—a yeoman.

It was quite another matter when one of the sons or daughters was guilty of misconduct; then he or she was struck out of the pedigree. I know of one or two little domestic scandals to which the registers bear witness, and I know that in such cases those who have stained the family name have not been recorded in the heralds' book. But that Joan who married a blacksmith, or Nicolas who was an armourer in London should be cancelled—God forbid!

My own conviction is, confirmed by a very close study of parochial registers, that some of the very best blood in England is to be found among the tradesmen of our county towns.

I know a little china and glass shop in the market-place of a small country town. The name over the shop is peculiar, but I know that it is one of considerable antiquity. In the reign of Henry VII. a Jewish refugee settled in Cornwall. His son, a barber-surgeon, prospered, and became Mayor of Liskeard. His children married well, mostly with families of county position, and a son settled in the

4

little town I speak of, where he married one of the honourable family of Edgecumbe. And now the lineal descendant of this man, in the male line, keeps a little china shop. I know—what perhaps he does not—his arms, crest, and motto, to which he has just claim.

Let us take another instance. When the lands of the Abbey of Tavistock were made over to the Russell family, on one of the largest farms or estates that belonged to the Abbey was seated a family that had been for a long time hereditary tenants under the Abbot. In the same position they continued, only under the Russells. In the reign of Elizabeth or of James I. they built themselves a handsome residence, with hall and mullioned windows, and laid out the grounds, and dug fish-ponds about this mansion. They also acquired lands of their own; amongst other estates a house that had belonged to the Speccots. They produced a sheriff of the county in the eighteenth century. As late as 1820 they were seated in their grand old mansion. Then—how I cannot tell— there came a collapse. They lost the house and lands they had held since the thirteenth century; the Duke of Bedford pulled down the house, and the family is now represented by a surgeon, a hairdresser, and a hatter. The coat of arms borne by this family is found in every book of heraldry, it is so remarkable—a woman's breast distilling milk.

Sir Bernard Burke, in his Vicissitudes of Families, tells the pathetic tale of the fall of the great baronial family of Conyers. The elder line became extinct in 1731, when the baronetcy fell to Ralph Conyers, Chester-le-street, a glazier, whose father, John, was grandson of the first Baronet. Sir Ralph intermarried with Jane Blackiston, the eventual heiress of the Blackistons of Shieldun, a family not less ancient. His eldest son, Sir Blackiston Conyers, the heir of two ancient houses, derived from them little more than his name. He went into the navy, where he reached the rank of lieutenant, and became on leaving the navy collector of the port of Newcastle. He died without a son, and his title and property went to his nephew, Sir George, whose mother was a lady of Lord Cathcart's family. In three years this young fellow squandered the property and died, leaving the barren title to his uncle, Thomas Conyers, who, after an unsuccessful attempt at a humble business, in his seventy-second year was residing as a pauper in the workhouse of Chester-le-Street.

Mr. Surtees bestirred himself in his favour, collected a little subscription, which enabled the old baronet to leave the workhouse. This was in 1810, and he died soon after, leaving three daughters married to labouring men in the little town of Chester-le-Street.

I have already mentioned the Coryndons of Bratton-Clovelly. It was a family not of splendour but of antiquity.

In 1620, when they registered their pedigree, they began with one Roger Coryndon, "who cam out of the Easterne parts and lived at Bratton neere 200 yeares since." There they remained till the beginning of this century, the property passing through the hands of a John Coryndon, barber of Exeter; a Thomas Coryndon, a tailor there; and George Coryndon, a wheelwright in Plymouth dockyard in 1748, whose son in a title-deed signs himself "gentleman," as he was perfectly justified in doing.

A family may be ruined by extravagance, but it is not always through ruin that the representatives it a family are to be found in humble or comparatively humble circumstances; but that the junior members of a gentle family went into trade. The occasion of that irruption of false pride relative to "soiling the hands with trade," was the great change that ensued after Queen Anne's reign. When the trade of the country grew, great fortunes were made in business, at the same time that the landed gentry had become impoverished, first through their losses in the Civil War, then by the extravagance of the period of the Restoration, together with drinking and gambling. Vast numbers of estates changed hands, passed away from the old aristocracy into the possession of men who had amassed fortunes in trade, and it was among the children of these rich retired tradesmen that there sprang up such a contempt for whatever savoured of the shop and the counting-house. I know a horse that had been wont to draw an apple-cart for an itinerant vendor of fruit. He had several admirable points about him, indications that showed he was qualified to make a good carriage-horse. He was bought by a dealer, and sold to a squire. Then he was groomed, put into silvered harness, and became a favourite with the ladies as a docile beast to drive in a low carriage. One day as his mistress was taking out a friend in the trap, she told her the story of the horse. At the word "apple-cart" back went the ears of the brute, and he kicked the carriage to pieces. After this it was quite sufficient to visit the stable and to mention "apple-cart" to set the horse kicking. Which story may be applied to what has been said about the nouveaux-riches of Queen Anne's time and trade.

It has often struck observers that wherever an important county family has resided for many generations, there are to be found among the poor many families bearing the same name, and it is rashly concluded that these are scions of the ancient stock.

It does so happen sometimes that these cottagers represent the old family, but only very rarely. Representatives are far more likely to be found as yeomen or tradesmen. The bearing of the name is no guarantee to filiation, even irregular; for it was by no means infrequent for servants to bear their masters' names; and the cottagers bearing the proud names of Courtenay, Berkley, Percy, Devereux, probably have not one drop of the noble blood of these families in their veins. But this is a subject to which I will return when speaking about old servants.

Now let us consider what was the origin of our county families.

Some have been estated, lords of manors, for many centuries, but these are few and far between. Then comes a whole class of men who worked themselves up from being yeomen, small owners into great owners, by thrift and moderation. I know some cases of small holders of land, who have held their little properties for three or four centuries, but who have never advanced in the social scale. Others have added field to field, have taken advantage of the improvidence of their neighbours, and have bought them out. Then they have risen to become gentry. But the most numerous class is that of the well-to-do merchants, who have bought lands and founded families. In my own county of Devon this is the history of the origin of a considerable number of those families which claimed a right to bear arms, and proved their pedigrees before the heralds at the beginning of the seventeenth century. Dartmouth, Totnes, Exeter, Bideford, Barnstaple—all the great commercial centres—saw the building up of county families. The same process which began in the reign of Elizabeth has continued to this day, and will continue so long as the possession of a country house and of acres proves attractive; and may it long so continue, for what else does this mean than the bringing of money into country places, and not of money only, but of intelligence, culture, and good fellowship?

One of the most extraordinary phenomena of social history in our land is the way in which the landed aristocracy have become extinct in the male line; how families of note have disappeared, as though engulfed like Korah and his company. Recklessness of living and ruin will not account for this. It is not that they have parted with their acres that surprises us, but the way in which the families have disappeared, as if snuffed out altogether.

It is feasible—I do not say easy—to trace a family of quite ordinary position with certainty through many generations. Whoever had any property made a will, or, if he neglected to make a will, had an administration of his effects taken by the next of kin after his death; and will or administration tell us about the man and where he lived. Then we refer to the parish registers, and with their assistance get some more information. There are other means by which additional matter may be acquired. Thus it is quite possible to draw a pedigree—a genuine, well-authenticated one—of almost any tradesman's or yeoman's family from the time of Elizabeth.

Now Lieutenant-Colonel Vivian has spent infinite pains in tracing the genealogies of those families in the West of England which bore arms, and were accounted gentle at the beginning of the seventeenth century down to the present day. For this purpose he has searched all the wills extant relative to Devon and Cornwall, and most of the parish registers in these counties. Consequently, we can take his conclusions as being as reliable as they can well be made.

In the sixteenth and seventeenth centuries the heralds made periodical visitations of the counties, and noted down the pedigrees of the gentle families, enrolled such as had a right to bear arms, and disqualified as ignobiles such as had assumed the position and arms of a gentleman without legitimate title.

In the county of Devon there were visitations by the heralds in 1531, 1564, 1572, and 1620, this last was the final visitation made. Now in the lists then drawn up appear fourteen gentle families under letter A, forty-seven under B, sixty-three under C.

Of the fourteen whose names began with A, the Aclands alone remain. Of the forty-seven whose names began with B, only five remain. Of the sixty-three under C, fifty-eight are gone. Some few linger on, represented in the female line, but such are not included, though the descendants may have taken the ancient name.

How are we to account for this amazing extinction? The families were prolific, but apparently those most prolific most rapidly exhausted their vitality.

The Arscotts go back to the beginning of the reign of Henry VI., and spread over the north of Devon. John Arscott of Arscott, who died in 1563, had eight sons. His eldest son Humphry had indeed but two, but of these, the eldest and heir had two, and the second had six; yet in 1634 the estates devolved on a daughter.

John Arscott in 1563 had three brothers. Of these the next, Thomas, married a Bligh in 1551, and had four sons. Of these the descendants of one alone can be traced to a certain Roseclear Arscott of Holsworthy, who left four sons; all these died without issue. The son and heir is buried at Whitchurch, near Tavistock, with the laconic entry—"Charles Arscott, gent., of age, but not worth £300; buried 23 March, 1704-5."

The third of the four—of whom John Arscott was the eldest—was Richard, who left four sons. Of these the second, Humphry, was the father of seven, and Tristram, the eldest, of two. Tristram's family died out in the male line in 1620. Of the seven sons of Humphry all traces have disappeared. The fourth was John Arscott of Tetcott, he, like his elder brothers, a man of good estate. His family became extinct in the male line in 1788.

The Crymes family, of Buckland Monachorum, was vastly prolific. William Crymes, who died in 1621, had nine sons; of these, as far as is known, only three married—William, Lewis, and Ferdinando. William left but one son; Lewis had a son who died in infancy, and that son only; Ferdinando had a son of the same name, whose only son died within a year of his birth. Ellis Crymes, the son of William, and inheritor of the estate, married twice, and had by his first wife, a daughter of Sir Francis Drake, as many as ten sons; by his second wife he had six more. Of the ten first only eight had children; and of the offspring of the second batch of six not a single grandchild male lived. In two generations after this prolific Ellis with his sixteen sons, the whole family disappears. I do not say that it is absolutely blotted out of the land of the living, but it is no longer represented in the county, nor can it be traced further.

I can give an excellent example in my own family, as I have taken great pains to trace all the ramifications. In the Visitation of 1620, John Gould of Coombe in Staverton is represented as father of seven sons; and Prince, who wrote his Worthies of Devon, published in 1701, in mentioning the family, comments on its great expansion; yet of all these sons, who, one would have supposed, would have half peopled the county, but a single male lineal representative remains, and he is over fifty, and unmarried.

The Heles were one of the most widely-spread and deeply-rooted families in the West of England. At an assize in Exeter in 1660, when Matthew Hele was high-sheriff, the entire grand-jury, numbering about twenty, was all composed of men of substance and quality, and all bearing the name of Hele. Where are they now? Vanished, root and branch.

Where are the Dynhams, once holding many lordships in Devon? Gone, leaving an empty shell—their old manor-house of Wortham—to show where they had been.

In the seventeenth century John Bridgeman, Bishop of Chester, father of Sir Orlando Bridgeman, and ancestor of the Earl of Bradford, bought the fine old mansion, Great Levers, that had at one time belonged to the Lever family, then had passed to the Ashtons. He reglazed his hall window, that was in four compartments, with coats of arms. In the first light he inserted the armorial bearings of the Levers, with the motto "Olim" (Formerly); in the next the arms of the Ashtons, with the legend, "Heri"

(Yesterday); then his own, with the text, "Hodie" (To-day); and he left the fourth and last compartment without a blazoning, but with the motto, "Cras, nescio cujus" (Whose to-morrow, I know not).

Possibly one reason for the extinction, or apparent extinction, of the squirarchal families is, that the junior branches did not keep up their connexion with the main family trunk, and so in time all reminiscence of cousinship disappeared; and yet, this is not so likely to have occurred in former times, when families held together in a clannish fashion, as at present.

When Charles, thirteenth Duke of Norfolk, had completed his restoration of Arundel Castle, he proposed to entertain all the descendants of his ancestor, Jock of Norfolk, who fell at Bosworth, but gave up the intention on finding that he would have to invite upwards of six thousand persons.

In the reign of James I., Lord Montague desired leave of the king to cut off the entail of some land that had been given to his ancestor, Sir Edward Montague, chief justice in the reign of Henry VIII., with remainder to the Crown; and he showed the king that it was most unlikely that it ever would revert to the Crown, as at that time there were alive four thousand persons derived from the body of Sir Edward, who died in 1556. In this case the noble race of Montague has lasted, and holds the Earldom of Sandwich, and the Dukedom and Earldom of Manchester. The name of Montague now borne by the holder of the Barony of Rokeby is an assumption, the proper family name being Robinson.

"When King James came into England," says Ward in his Diary, "he was feasted at Boughton by Sir Edward Montague, and his six sons brought up the six first dishes. Three of them were lords, and three more knights."

Fuller in his Worthies records that "Hester Sandys, the wife of Sir Thomas Temple, of Stowe, Bart., had four sons and nine daughters, which lived to be married, and so exceedingly multiplied, that she saw seven hundred extracted from her body," yet—what became of the Temples? The estate of Stowe passed out of the male line with Hester, second daughter of Sir Richard Temple, who married Richard Grenville, and she was created Countess Temple with limitation to the heirs male of her body. There is at present a (Sir) Grenville Louis John Temple, great-great-grandson to (Sir) John Temple, who in 1786 assumed the baronetcy conferred upon Sir Thomas Temple of Stowe in 1611. This (Sir) John, who was born at Boston, in the United States, assumed the baronetcy on the receipt of a letter from the then Marquis of Buckingham, informing him of the death of Sir Richard Temple in 1786; but the heirship has not been proved, and there exists a doubt whether the claim can be substantiated.[1]

Innocent XIII. (1721-4) boasted that he had nine uncles, eight brothers, four nephews, and seven grandnephews. He thought, and others thought with him, that the Conti family was safe to spread and flourish. Yet, a century later, and not a Conti remained.

In the following chapter I will tell the story of the extinction of a family that was of consequence and wealth in the West of England, owning a good deal of land at one time. The story is not a little curious, and as all the particulars are known to me, I am able to relate it with some minuteness. It affords a picture of a condition of social life sufficiently surprising, and at a period by no means remote.

---

[1] Foster, Baronetage, 1880. See Chaos, p. 653.

CHAPTER II

THE LAST SQUIRE

IN a certain wild and picturesque region of the west, which commands a noble prospect of Dartmoor, in a small but antique mansion, which we will call Grimstone, lived for generations a family called Grym. This family rose to consequence after the last heralds' visitation, consequently did not belong to the aboriginal gentry of the county. It produced a chancellor, and an Archbishop of Canterbury.

The family mansion is still standing, with granite mullioned windows and quaint projecting porch, over which is a parvise. A pair of carved stone gate-posts give access to the turf plot in front of the house. The mighty kitchen with three fireplaces shows that the Gryms were a hospitable race, who would on high days feed a large number of guests, and the ample cellars show that they did more than feed them. I cannot recall any library in the house, unless, perhaps, the porch-room were intended for books; if so, it continued to be intended for them only.

The first man of note in the family who lived at Grimstone was Brigadier John Grym of the Guards, born in 1699, a fine man and a gallant soldier. He had one son, of the same name as himself, a man amiable, weakly in mind, and of no moral force and decision of character. His father and mother were a little uneasy about him because he was so infirm of purpose; they put their heads together, and concluded that the best thing to do for him was to marry him to a woman who had in abundance those qualities in which their son was deficient. Now there lived about four miles off, in a similar quaint old mansion, a young lady of very remarkable decision of character. She was poor, and one of a large family. She at once accepted the offer made her in John Grym's name by the Brigadier and his wife, and became Madame John Grym, and on the death of the Brigadier, Madame Grym, and despotic reigning queen of Grimstone, who took the reins of government into her firm hands, and never let them out of them. The saying goes, when woman drives she drives to the devil, and madame did not prove an exception.

The marriage had taken place in 1794; the husband died six years later, but madame survived till 1835. Throughout the minority of her eldest son John, that is to say, for sixteen or seventeen years, she had the entire, uncontrolled management of the property, and she managed pretty well in that time to ruin the estate.

She was a litigious woman, always at strife with her neighbours, proud and ambitious. Her ambition was to extend the bounds of the property, but she had not the capital to dispose of to enable her to pay for the lands she purchased, and which were mortgaged to two-thirds of their value. She borrowed money at five and six per cent., and bought property with it that rendered only three and a half.

She attended the parish vestries, where she made her will felt, and pursued with implacable animosity such farmers or landowners as did not submit to her dictation. She drove a pair of ponies herself, but whilst driving had her mind so engaged in her schemes that she forgot to attend to the beasts; they sometimes ran away with her, upset her, and she was found on more than one occasion senseless by the roadside, and her carriage shattered hard by.

As her affairs became worse, more and more intricately involved, she began to be alarmed lest she should be arrested for debt. For security she had a house or pavilion erected in which to take refuge should the officers of the law come for her. This had a secret chamber, or well, made in the thickness of the walls, accessible from an upper loft through a trap-door. When she had received warning that she was being looked for, she fled to the loft. The trap was raised, and madame was lowered into the well on a carpet or sheet, then the trap was closed and covered with a mat. She had recourse to this place of concealment on several occasions, and the secret of the hiding-nest was not revealed till after her death.

The pavilion still stands, but has been converted into a barn, and all the internal arrangements have been altered.

When defeated in an action against a neighbour, on success in which she had greatly set her heart, she brought an action against the lawyer who had conducted her case, charging him with having wilfully understated her claims, withheld evidence, and acted in collusion with the other side. She lost, of course, and being unable to pay costs, escaped to London; there she died. It is said that when the judgment was given against her the church bells were rung, so unpopular had she become.

In London she died, and her son, fearing lest her body should be arrested for debt, had her packed in bran, in a grand-piano case, and sent down by water to Plymouth, whence it was conveyed by waggon, as a piano, to Grimstone. The bill for the packing of madame in bran in a piano case is still extant. The waggoner who drove her in this case from Plymouth did not die till the other day.

At the time when she was in constant alarm of a warrant and execution, the portable plate of the house, to the weight of about fifty pounds, was daily intrusted to one of the labourers on the farm, who carried it about with him, and when at work put it in the hedge, and threw his jacket over it.

On one occasion, when the bailiffs were expected, she was afraid lest her gig should be taken, and before retiring into her well, she had it lifted by ropes and concealed under hay above the stable.

She left two sons, John, the elder, the heir to Grimstone, and Ralph, the younger. Both inherited the self-will, strength of character, and vindictiveness of the mother, but the younger assuredly in double measure. No sooner was she dead, than the brothers flew at each other's throats, or, to be more exact, Ralph flew at that of his more fortunate brother, if it can be called fortunate to inherit an encumbered estate, mortgaged almost to its value. Ralph instituted a Chancery suit against John. The younger brother remained in the parish, residing in another house, and occasionally accompanied his brother John when out shooting, and they met in the hunting-field.

One day when they were out rabbiting together, Ralph's gun suddenly went off, and riddled his brother's beaver hat. John vowed that a deliberate attempt had been made on his life by his brother. He forbade him his house, and thenceforth would no more associate with him in field sports. Ralph before his mother's death had been put in a solicitor's office, but had been dismissed from it for falling on a fellow-clerk with a pistol and attempting to shoot him. John remembered this, and if he mistrusted his brother, it was not altogether without cause.

Now that he could no longer go to Grimstone, and found himself regarded askance by the neighbours, Ralph went up to town, where, having connexions in good position, he got introduced into society, and he made the acquaintance of a very charming girl with a small fortune at her own disposal, of six thousand pounds. He was a remarkably handsome young man, with flashing blue eyes, and bold, well-chiselled features, an erect bearing, and a brusque, haughty manner. It is perhaps hardly to be wondered at that, with his personal good looks, and with his indomitable will, he should bear down all opposition on the part of the young lady's friends, and induce her to throw in her lot with him.

According to the marriage settlement, half the wife's fortune was to be at his disposal. It is almost unnecessary to say, that he managed to get rid of that within a twelvemonth. Thereupon ensued a series of persecutions as mean as they were cruel. His object was to force her to surrender the second three thousand pounds. He attempted to cajole her out of this, and when he failed by this means, he endeavoured to frighten her into submission. To do this he put a pistol under the pillow, and when she was asleep at his side, discharged the pistol over her head. Then he pretended that he had missed his mark, but assured her he would not fail another time.

She had, fortunately, sufficient resolution to resist intimidation. Whether she would have succumbed in the end we cannot say, but, luckily for her, he was arrested for costs in the Chancery suit against his brother, and was lodged in the prison of King's Bench, where he remained for seven years. Bethell, afterwards Lord Westbury, was counsel against him. Ralph Grym conducted his own case. Every now and then he was brought from prison into court, as some fresh stage of the case was entered upon, and then returned to his detention. One day Bethell informed the judge that he moved for an "abatement," owing to the death of one of the parties involved in the suit. This was the first tidings Ralph Grym received of the decease of his brother-in-law, who with his brother John was party in the suit. His brother now abandoned the action, and Ralph was let out of King's Bench. He at once returned to the neighbourhood of Grimstone, and sent a message to his brother on the very first night of his return that he had a gun; that he was passionately fond of shooting; that for seven or eight years he had been debarred the pleasure; that his hand had become shaky; and that—in all human probability, when he was out shooting, should John come in sight, his gun would go off accidentally, and on this occasion not perforate the beaver.

John took the hint and remained indoors, whilst Ralph shot when and what he liked over his brother's grounds. But this was a condition of affairs so intolerable, that John deemed it expedient to come to terms with his brother, give him five hundred pounds, and pack him off to London.

Furnished with this sum, Ralph returned to town, and there set up livery stables. He was himself a first-rate rider, and he taught ladies riding, and conducted riding parties in Epping forest. He made money by purchasing good-looking horses that were faulty in one or two particulars, at some ten pounds or fifteen pounds, and as his horses were well turned out, and well bred, he had the credit of mounting his customers well. And he was not indisposed to sell some of these for very considerable sums.

Thus passed three or four years, the happiest in his life, and he might have continued his livery stables, had he not quarrelled

15

with a groom and fought him. He was thrown, and dislocated his hip. This was badly set; it was a long job, and he was never again able to ride comfortably. His business went back, he lost his customers, and failed. Then, without a penny in his pocket, he returned to Devon, and to the neighbourhood of Grimstone, and lodged with the tenants on the estate.

Utterly ruined in means and in credit, he became a burden to his hosts. They declined to entertain him wholly and severally, so he slept in one farmhouse, and had his meals in one or another of the neighbouring farms. His brother refused to see him, defied his threats, and denied him money.

This went on for some time. At length his hosts plainly informed him that he was no longer welcome. He was not an agreeable guest, was exacting, insolent, and violent. They met in consultation, sent round the hat, collected a small subvention; and then a gig was got ready, the money thrust into his hand, and he was mounted in the trap to be driven off to the nearest railway station, where he might take a ticket for London, or Jericho. The gig was at the door, and Ralph was settling himself into it, when a man, breathless and without a hat, arrived running from Grimstone, to say that John Grym, his brother, had suddenly fallen down dead. The trap that was to take Ralph away now conveyed him to the mansion of his ancestors, to take possession as heir, and he carried off with him the proceeds of the subscription among the tenants.

John had died without issue, and intestate. Ralph found in the house five hundred pounds in gold, a thousand pounds' worth of stock was on the farm, three hundred pounds' worth of wool was in store, and there was much family plate and some family jewels.

Ralph's character from this moment underwent a change. When in town he had lived as a prodigal, and squandered his money as it came in, was freehanded and genial. In the year of Bloomsbury, when the Derby was run in snow, he won three thousand pounds by a bet, when he had not three-halfpence of his own. Next year he won on the turf fifteen hundred pounds; but money thus made slipped through his fingers. No sooner, however, was he squire of Grimstone than he became a miser, and that so suddenly, that he had to be sued in the County Court for the cheap calico he had ordered for a shroud for his brother. He became the hardest of landlords and the harshest of masters.

With his wife he was not reconciled. Repeated efforts were made by well-intentioned persons to re-unite them. He protested his willingness to receive her, but only on the condition that she made over to him the remaining three thousand pounds of her property. To this condition she had the wisdom not to accede. Before he was imprisoned she had borne him a daughter, whom we will call Rosalind. He made many attempts to get possession of the child, in the hopes of thereby extorting the money from the mother.

Before he became squire, Mrs. Grym lived in a small house near Grimstone, on the interest of the three thousand pounds, of course in a very small way. On one occasion she was called to town, and was unable to take little Rosalind with her. She accordingly conveyed the child to the house of a neighbouring rector, and entreated that she might be kept there till her return, and be on no account surrendered to the father should he attempt to claim her.

A couple of Sundays after her departure, between ten and eleven in the morning, Ralph Grym appeared at the parsonage, and asked to see the rector. He was admitted, and after a little preliminary conversation, stated his desire to have an interview with his child, then aged five. This could not be refused. The little girl was introduced, and Ralph talked to her, and played with her.

In the meantime the bells for service were ringing. The bell changed to the last single toll, five minutes before divine worship began, and Mr. Grym made no signs of being in a hurry to depart.

The rector, obliged to attend to his sacred duties, drew his son aside, a boy of sixteen, and said to him, "Harry, keep your eye on Rosalind, and on no account suffer Mr. Grym to carry her off."

The boy accordingly remained at home.

"Well, young shaver," said Ralph, "what are you staying here for?"

"My father does not wish me to go to church this morning."

"Rosalind," said her father, "go, fetch your bonnet, and come a walk with me. I have some peppermints in my pocket."

The child, highly elated, got herself ready. Henry, the rector's son, also prepared to go out.

"Young shaver, we don't want you," said Ralph, rudely.

"My father ordered me to take a walk this morning, sir."

"There are two ways—I and Rosalind go one, and you the other," said Ralph.

"My father bade me on no account leave Rosalind."

Ralph growled and went on, the boy following. Mr. Grym led the way for six miles, and the child became utterly wearied. The father made every effort to shake off the boy. He swore at him, he threatened him, money he had not got to offer him; all was in vain. At last, when the little girl sat down exhausted, and began to cry, the father with an oath left her.

"That," said Henry, in after life, "was the first time I had to do with Ralph Grym, and then I beat him."

Many years after he had again to stand as Rosalind's protector against Ralph, then striking at his child with a dead hand, and again he beat him.

After her mother's death Ralph invited his daughter to Grimstone, but only with the object of extorting from her the three thousand pounds she had inherited from her mother. When she refused to surrender this, he let her understand that her presence was irksome to him. He shifted the hour of dinner from seven to nine, then to ten, and finally gave orders that no dinner was to be served for a week. Still she did not go.

"I want your room, Rosalind," he said roughly; "I have a friend coming."

"The house is large, there are plenty of apartments; he shall have mine, I will move into another."

"I want all the rooms."

"I see you want to drive me away."

"I beg you will suit yourself as to the precise hour to-morrow when you leave."

Again, after some years, was Rosalind invited to Grimstone; but it was with the same object, never abandoned. On this occasion, when old Ralph found that she was resolute not to surrender the three thousand pounds, he turned her out of doors at night, and she was forced to take refuge at the poor little village tavern. He never forgave her.

Squire Grym was rough to his tenants. One man, the village clerk, had a field of his, and Ralph suddenly demanded of him two pounds above the rent the man had hitherto paid. As he refused, Ralph abruptly produced a horse-pistol, presented it at the man's head, and said,

"Put down the extra two pounds, or I will blow your brains out."

The clerk was a sturdy fellow, and was undaunted. He looked the squire steadily in the eye, and answered—

"I reckon her (i. e. the pistol), though old and risty, won't miss, for if her does, I reckon your brains 'll make a purty mess on the carpet."

Ralph lowered the pistol with an oath, and said no more. He was a suspicious man, and fancied that all those about him conspired to rob him. When he bore a grudge against a man, or suspected him, he required some of his tenants to give evidence against the man; he himself prepared the story they were to swear to, and drilled them into the evidence they were to give. The tenant who refused to do as he bid was never forgiven.

He was never able to keep a bailiff over a twelvemonth. When he died, at an age over eighty, in his vindictiveness against his daughter, because she had refused him the three thousand pounds, he left everything of which he was possessed to the bailiff then in his house. How the boy who had saved Rosalind from being carried off by her father many years before, and who was now a solicitor, came to her aid, and secured for her something out of the spoils, is history too recent to be told here.

Thus ended the family of Grym of Grimstone, and thus did the old house and old acres pass away into new hands.

Such is the story of the extinction of one family. Others have been snuffed out, or have snuffed themselves out, in other ways; strangely true it is, that of the multitudes of old county families that once lived in England, few remain on their paternal inheritance.

As I have told the story of the ruin of one family, I will conclude this chapter with that of the saving of another when trembling on the brink of ruin. Again I will give fictitious names. The St. Pierres were divided into two main branches, the one seated on a considerable estate on the Dart, near Ashburton, the other on a modest property near the Tamar, on the Devonshire side. In 1736 died Edward St. Pierre, the last male representative of the elder branch, when he left his property to the representative of the junior, William Drake St. Pierre. This latter had an only son, Edward, and a daughter. He was married to a woman of considerable force of character. On his death in 1766, Edward, then aged twenty-six, came in for a very large property indeed; he was in the Dragoons, and a dare-devil, gambling fellow. He eloped with a married lady, and lived with her for some years. She died, and was buried at Bath Abbey. He never married, but continued his mad career till his death.

One day he had been gambling till late, and had lost every guinea he had about him. Then he rode off, put a black mask over his face, and waylaid the man who had won the money of him, and on his appearance challenged him to deliver. The man recognized him, and incautiously exclaimed, "Oh, Edward St. Pierre! I did not think this of you!"

"You know me, do you?" was the reply, and Edward St. Pierre shot him dead.

Now there had been a witness, a man who had seen Captain Edward take up his position, and who, believing him to be a highwayman, had secreted himself, and waited his time to escape.

Edward St. Pierre was tried for the murder. Dunning of Ashburton, then a rising lawyer, was retained to defend him. It was essential to weaken or destroy the testimony of the witness. Dunning had recourse to an ingenious though dishonest device. The murder had been committed when the moon was full, or nearly full, so that in the brilliant white light every object was as clear as by day.

Dunning procured a pocket almanack, removed the sheet in which was the calendar of the month of the murder, and had it reprinted at the same press, or at all events with exactly similar type, altering the moons, so as to make no moon on the night in question.

On the day of trial he left this almanack in his great-coat pocket, hanging up in the ante-room of the court. The trial took place, and the witness gave his evidence.

"How could you be sure that the man on horseback was Captain St. Pierre?" asked the judge.

"My Lord, the full moon shone on him. I knew his horse; I knew his coat. Besides, when he had shot the other he took off his mask."

"The full moon was shining, do you say?"

"Yes, my Lord; I saw his face by the clear moonlight."

"Pass me a calendar. Who has got a calendar?" asked the judge.

At that time almanacks were not so plentiful as they are now. As it happened no one present had one. Then Dunning stood up, and said,—

"My Lord, I had one yesterday, and I put it, I think, in the pocket of my overcoat. If your Lordship will send an apparitor into the ante-room to search my pocket, it may there be found."

The calendar was produced—there was no moon. The evidence against the accused broke down, and he was acquitted.

This was considered at the time a clever move of Mr. Dunning; it occurred to no one that it was immoral. Captain St. Pierre had to pay Dunning heavily; in fact, he made over to him a portion of the estate in lieu of paying in cash, and later, when he became further involved, he sold the property to the Barings. Dunning was created Baron Ashburton, but the title became extinct with his son, who bequeathed his property to Alexander Baring, his first cousin, who was elevated to the peerage under the title of Baron Ashburton, and the St. Pierre property now belongs to Lord Ashburton.

Captain Edward St. Pierre died in 1788, without issue, and his sister became his heir; but he had got rid of everything he could get rid of. Only the estate near the Tamar had been saved from sale by his mother taking it of him on a lease for ninety-nine years. She was residing on it when the news reached her that her good-for-nothing son was dead.

He had died at Shaldon, near Teignmouth, on the 29th June, and his last request was that he might be carried to Bath, and laid by the side of the woman he had wronged.

When his mother received the tidings of his death she was in uncertainty what to do. All the last night of June to the dawn of July 1, she sat in one tall-backed arm-chair, musing what to do with the rest of her life. Should she go to Bath, and spend the remainder of her days at cards, amusing herself? or should she devote it to a country life, and to repairing the shattered fortunes of the family?

When morning broke her mind was made up. She would adopt the nobler, the better cause; and she carried it out to the end. As each farm fell vacant in the parish she took it into her own hands, and farmed it herself, and succeeded so well, that when the rival gentle family in the parish, owning a handsome barton there, fell into difficulties, she bought their estate, so as to make some amends for the loss of the Ashburton property. That the chair in which the old lady sat meets with respect ça va sans dire.

CHAPTER III

COUNTRY HOUSES

WHAT a feature in English scenery is the old country house! Compare the seat that has been occupied for many generations with the new mansion. The former with its embowering trees, its lawns and ancient oaks, its avenues of beech, the lofty, flaky Scotch pines in which the rooks build, and about which they wheel and caw; and the latter with new plantations, the evidence everywhere present of hedges pulled down, manifest in the trees propped up on hunches of clay.

There is nothing so striking to the eye on a return to England from the Continent as the stateliness of our trees. I do not know of any trees in Europe to compare with ours. It is only with us that they are allowed to grow to advanced age, and die by inches; only with us are they given elbow-room to expand into the full plenitude of their growth. On the Continent every tree is known to the police, when it was planted, when it attains its maximum of growth; and then, down it comes.

Horace Walpole had no love of the country—indeed, he hated it, and regarded the months that he spent in Norfolk as intolerable. He laments in a letter to Sir Horace Mann (Oct. 3rd, 1743), that the country houses of the nobility and gentry of England are scattered about in the country, and are not moved up to town, where they would make streets of palaces, like those of the great people of Florence, and Genoa, and Bologna. "Think what London would be if the chief houses were in it, as in the cities of other countries, and not dispersed, like great rarity-plums in a vast pudding of country."

It is precisely because our most noble mansions are in the country, in a setting of their own, absolutely incomparable, of park and grove, that they are unsurpassed for loveliness anywhere. Framed in by pines and deciduous trees, copper beech and silver poplar, with shrubberies of azalea in every range of colour, from scarlet, through yellow to white, and rhododendrons full of bloom from early spring to midsummer, and double cherry, almond, medlar. Why, the very framing makes an ugly country house look sweet and homelike.

But beautiful as are the parks and grounds about our gentlemen's houses, they are but a remnant of what once was. We see in our old churches, in our mansions, that oak grew in profusion

22

in England at one time, and reached sizes we cannot equal now. Great havoc was wrought with the woods and parks in the time of the Commonwealth and at the Restoration. The finest trees were cut down that ships might be built of them for the royal navy; the commissioners marked and took what trees they would. Thus in 1664 Pepys had to select trees in Clarendon Park, near Salisbury, which the Chancellor had bought of the Duke of Albemarle. Very angry the Chancellor was at having his park despoiled of his best timber, and Pepys gives us in his Diary an amusing account of his trouble thereupon.

But to come to the houses themselves. Is there anything more sweet, peaceful, comfortable than the aspect of an old country house, of brick especially, with brown tiled roof and clustering chimneys backed by woods, with pleasure gardens at its side, and open lawn and park before it? No, its equal is to be found nowhere. The French château, the Italian palace, the German schloss are not to be spoken of in the same breath. Each has its charm, but there is a coldness and stiffness in the first, a turned-inwardness in the second, and a nakedness in the last that prevent us from associating with them the ideas of comfort and peace.

The true English country house is a product of comparatively late times, that is to say, from the reign of Henry VIII. onwards. Before that, the great nobles lived in castles, and the smaller gentry in houses of no great comfort and grandeur.

In the parish of Little Hempston, near Totnes, is a perfect mansion of the fourteenth century, probably the original manor-house of the Arundels, but given to the Church, when it became a parsonage. It is now used as a farm, and a very uncomfortable farm-house it makes. As one of the best preserved houses of that period I know, it deserves a few words.

This house consists of three courts; one is a mere garden court, through which access was had to the main entrance; through this passed the way into the principal quadrangle. The third court was for stables and cattle-sheds. Now this house has but a single window in it looking outwards, and that is the great hall window, all the rest look inwards into the tiny quadrangle, which is almost like a well, never illumined by the sun, so small is it.

The hall had in it a brazier in the midst, which could never heat it, though the numbed fingers might be thawed at it. Adjoining the hall is the ladies' bower, a sitting-room dark as a vault, with indeed a fireplace in it. These were the sole rooms that were occupied by day, the hall and the bower.

The Arundels had another place at Ebbfleet, near Stratton,

which was no bigger, and only a little less gloomy; the windows were always made, for protection, to look into a court. It was not till after the Wars of the Roses that there was more light allowed into the chambers.

I give a sketch and plan of a manor-house still almost unaltered, called Willsworthy, in the parish of Peter Tavy in Devon. It is built entirely of granite. It has near it a ruined chapel, but what family occupied it and when I do not know; it has not certainly been tenanted by gentlefolks since the reign of Henry VIII.

It was not till the Tudor period that the houses of our forefathers became comfortable and cheerful.

We should be wrong, however, if we supposed that in the Elizabethan period the windows were designed so much for looking out at as for letting the sun look in at. The old idea of a quadrangle was not discarded, but it was modified. The quadrangle became a pleasant garden within walls; the destruction of the walls to afford vistas was the work of a later age.

The normal plan of a house till the reign of Elizabeth was the quadrangle; but then, in the more modest mansions, the house itself did not occupy more than a single side of the court, all the rest was taken up with barns and stables, and the windows of the house looked into this great stable-yard. On the side of Coxtor, above Tavistock, stands an interesting old yeoman's house, built of solid granite, which has remained in the possession of the same worthy family for many generations, and has remained unaltered. This house, in little, shows us the disposition of the old squire's mansion, for the yeoman copied the plan of the house of the lord of the manor. A granite doorway gives admission to the court, surrounded on all sides but the north by stabling. On the north side, raised above the yard by a flight of steps, is a small terrace laid out in flower-beds; into this court all the windows of the house look. We enter the porch, and find ourselves in the hall, with its great fireplace, its large south window, where sits the mistress at her needlework, as of old; and here is the high table, the wall panelled and carved, where sit the yeoman and his family at meals, whilst the labourers sit below. This very simple yet interesting house is quite a fortress; it is walled up against the stormy gales that sweep the moor. It is a prison too, for it catches and holds captive the sunbeams that fall into the bright little court.

We are too ready to regard our forefathers as fools, but they knew a thing or two; they were well aware that in England, if we want flowers to blow early and freely, they must be sheltered.

It was not till the reign of Charles II. that the fancy came on

English people to do away with nooks and corners, and to build oblong blocks of houses without projections anywhere.

The new Italian, or French château style, had its advantages, but its counterbalancing disadvantages. The main advantage was that the rooms were loftier than before; the walls, white and gold, were more cheerful at night; there may have been other advantages, but these are the only two that are conspicuous. The disadvantages were many. In the first place, no shelter was provided out of doors from the wind; no pleasant nooks, no sun-traps. The block of building, naked and alone, stood in the midst of a park, and the wind whistled round it, and the rain drove against it. When the visitor arrived in bad weather, he was blown in at the door, and nearly blown through the hall. In our eagerness to make vistas, obtain extensive landscapes, we have levelled our enclosing walls. But what could have been a sweeter prospect from a hall or parlour window, than an enclosed garden full of flowers, with bees humming, butterflies flitting, and fruit-trees ripening their burdens against old red brick enclosing walls, tinted gorgeously with lichens?

There is at present a fashion for being blown about by the wind, so we unmuffle our mansions of their enclosing walls and hedges. But England is a land of wind. Nothing strikes an Englishman more, when living abroad, than the general stillness of the air. Look at the wonderful bulbous spires and cupolas to towers on the Continent;—marvellously picturesque they are. If examined, they are found to be very generally covered with the most delicate slate work, that folds in and out of the crinks and crannies, like chain mail. Such slating would not endure three winters in England; it would be torn adrift and scattered like autumn leaves before an equinoctial gale. We never had these bulbous spires in England, because the climate would not permit of their construction. Our forefathers knew that this was a windy world of ours—

"Sing heigh ho for the wind and the rain,
For the rain it raineth every day,"

and they built their houses accordingly—to provide the greatest possible amount of shelter from the cold blasts of March, and from the driving rains of winter. The house originally consisted on the ground-floor of hall, parlour, kitchen, and entrance-porch and stairs. In later times the side wing was carried further back, and a second parlour was built, and the staircase erected between the parlours.

25

At Upcott, in Broadwood, in Devon, is a house that belonged to the Upcotts. The plan is much the same as that of Willsworthy, even ruder, though the house itself was finer. It had a porch, a hall, and a dairy and kitchen. The parlour is of Queen Anne's reign, and probably takes the place of one earlier on the same spot. The plan of Hurlditch is the same, a mansion of the important family of Speccot. There also the parlour is comparatively recent.

There was in a house previous to the reign of Henry VII. but one good room, and that was the hall. It opened to the roof, and must have been cold enough in winter, and draughty at all times.

At Wortham, the fine mansion of the Dynhams, there was an arrangement, as far as I know, unique—two halls, one for winter with a fire-place in it, serving as a sort of lower story to the summer-hall, clear to the roof—thus one is superposed on the other.

Tonacombe, a mansion of the Leys and Kempthornes in Morwenstowe parish in Cornwall, is a singularly untouched house of a somewhat similar construction, but enlarged. Here there was the tiny entrance-court into which the hall looked; the hall itself being open to the roof, with its great fire-place, and the parlour panelled with oak. All other reception-rooms are later additions or alterations of offices into parlours.

With the reign of the Tudors a great sense of security and an increase of wealth must have come to the country gentry, for they everywhere began to rebuild their houses, to give them more air and light, and completely shook off that fear which had possessed them previously of looking out into the world. Then came in an age of great windows. It would seem as though in the rebound they thought they could not have light enough. Certainly glass must have been inexpensive in those days. It was the same in the churches; the huge perpendicular windows converted the sacred edifices into lanterns. The old halls open to the roof gave way to ceiled halls, and the newel staircase in the wall—very inconvenient, impossible for the carrying up or down-stairs of large furniture—was discarded for the broad and stately staircase of oak.

It seems to me that the loss of shelter that ensued on the abandonment of the quadrangle, or of the E-shaped Elizabethan house, is not counterbalanced by the compactness of the square or the oblong block of the Queen Anne house. Moreover, the advantages internally were not so great as might be supposed, for, to light the very lofty room the windows were made narrow and tall; thus shaped they admitted far less sun than when they were broad and not tall.

Only one who, like myself, has the happiness to occupy a

room with a six-light window, twelve feet wide and five feet high, through which the sun pours in and floods the whole room, whilst without the keen March wind is cutting, cold and cruel, can appreciate the blessedness of such a window, can tell the exhilarating effect it has on the spirits, how it lets the sun in, not only through the room, and on to one's book or paper, but into the very heart and soul as well.

A long upright narrow window does not answer the purpose for which it was constructed. The light enters the room from the sky, not from the earth, therefore only through the upper portion of a window. The wide window gives us the greatest possible amount of light. If we were but to revert to the Elizabethan window, we would find a singular improvement in our health and spirits.

Our old country houses were, say modern masons, shockingly badly built. "Why, sir," said one to me, "do look here at this wall. It is three foot six thick—what waste of room!—and then only the facing is with mortar between the stones, all the rest of the stones are set in clay." I was engaged building my porch when the man said this. So I, convinced by his superior experience, apologized for my forbears, and bade him rebuild with mortar throughout. What was the result? That wall has been to me ever since a worry. The rain beats through it; every course of mortar serves as an aqueduct, and the driving rain against that wall traverses it as easily as if it were a sponge. Our old houses were dry within—dry as snuff. Now we cannot keep the wet out without cementing them externally. Those fools, our forefathers, by breaking the connexion prevented the water from penetrating.

Do any of my readers know the cosiness of an oak-panelled or of a tapestried room? There is nothing comparable to it for warmth. What the reader certainly does know is, that from a papered wall and from a plate-glass window there is ever a cold current of air setting inwards. He supposes that there is a draught creeping round the walls from the door, or that the window-frame does not fit; and he plugs, but cannot exclude the cold air. But the origin of the draught is in the room itself, and it is created by the fire. The wall is cold and the plate-glass is cold, and the heated atmosphere of the room is lowered in temperature against these cold surfaces, and returns in the direction of the fire as a chill draught. But when the room is lined with oak or with woven woollen tapestry, then the walls are warm, and they give back none of these chill recoil currents. The fire has not the double obligation laid on it of heating the air of the apartment and the walls.

In Germany and Russia during the winter double windows are

set up in every room, and by this means a film of warm air is interposed between the heated atmosphere of the room and the external cold air. That our ancestors did not attempt,—plate-glass was not known to them,—but they did what they could in the right direction. They covered the chill stone and plaster walls of the rooms with non-conducting materials.

The oak-panelled room was, it can hardly be denied, difficult to light at night, as the dark walls absorbed the candle rays. But that mattered little at a time when every one went to bed with the sun. When later hours were kept, then the oak panels were painted white. But now that we have mineral oils, not to mention gas and electric lighting, we may well scrape off the white paint and restore the dark oak. Then, for an evening, the sombre background has quite a marvellous effect in setting off the bright ladies' dresses, and showing off fresh pretty faces.

Before the reign of Elizabeth the staircase was not an important feature in the house. The hall reached to the roof, and the stairs were winding flights of stone steps in turrets, or in the thickness of the wall; when the fashion set in to ceil the halls low, then the staircase became a stately feature of the house. But it was more than a stately feature, it was the great ventilating shaft of the house; it was to the house what the tower is to the church, the chimney by which the stale fumes might pass away. The great staircase window, made up of thousands of little pieces of glass set in lead, acted as a colander through which the outer air streamed in and the inner vitiated air escaped. Where there is a central quadrangle, this was in many cases glazed in; then a staircase led to a series of galleries about it, lighted from above, communicating with the several suites of apartments. Many of our old inns are thus constructed. The reader will remember the picture of the court of the White Hart in Pickwick, with the first introduction of Sam Weller. The central court serves as a ventilator to the house, and so does its dwindled representative, the well-staircase. Those fools, our forefathers, again, if they shut out the winds and gave shelter to their houses, made ample provision for internal ventilation.

What a degraded, miserable feature of the house is the staircase now-a-days, with its steps seven inches instead of four, and the tread nine and a half inches instead of thirteen. It takes an effort to go up-stairs now, it is a scramble; it was an easy, a leisurely, and a dignified ascent formerly. Then again, our staircases are narrow—one of four feet is of quite a respectable width; but the old Elizabethan staircase measured from six feet to eight feet wide. That of Blickling Hall, Norfolk is seven feet eight inches. There the ascent is single to the first landing; after that the stair branches off, one for the ascent, the other for the descent. The first ascent is of eight steps; then after the main landing, on each side eleven steps to the second landing; then nine more lead to the level of the upper storys and grand corridor. On such staircases as these furniture can be conveyed up and down without damage to the walls, or injury to the furniture. Architects who build modern narrow and steep staircases, forget that often a coffin has to be conveyed with its tenant down them; and this can be done neither with convenience nor dignity upon them.

But let us think of the staircase on a brighter occasion than a funeral. The grand old flight of steps with its landings, and with sometimes its bay-window with seats in it on one of the landings, how it lends itself to the exigencies of a sitting-out place at a ball. The window is filled with azaleas; the walls hung with full-length family portraits; the broad dark oak stairs are carpeted with crimson; a chandelier pendant from the moulded Elizabethan ceiling-drop sheds a soft golden light over the scene; and on the landings, on the steps themselves, sit the dancers after the exertions of a waltz or a galop, enjoying the fresher air, and forming a picture of almost ideal charm. Then also it is that the ventilating advantages of the great staircase become most manifest. The dancing has been in the hall, which has become hot; the door on to the stairs is thrown open; there is a circulation of air at once, and in two minutes the atmosphere of the ball-room has renewed itself.

In the matter of sleeping arrangements we have certainly made an advance on those of our ancestors. I have already mentioned Upcott, which belonged to a family of that name that expired in the reign of Henry VII. The hall is small, but has a huge fire-place in it. In the window is a coat of arms, in stained glass, representing Upcott impaling an unknown coat, party per pale, argent and sable, three dexter hands couped at the wrist, counterchanged. Now this house has or had but a single bedroom. There may have been, and there probably was, a separate apartment for the squire and his wife, over the parlour, which was rebuilt later; but for all the rest of the household there existed but one large dormitory over the hall, in which slept the unmarried ladies of the family, and the maid-servants, and where was the nursery for the babies. All the men of the family, gentle and serving, slept in the hall about the fire on the straw, and fern, and broom that littered the pavement.

That house is a very astonishing one to me, for it reveals a state of affairs singularly rude—at a comparatively late period.

Things were improved in this particular later; bedrooms many were constructed, communicating with each other. At the head of the stairs slept the squire and his wife, and all the rooms tenanted by the rest of the household were accessible only through that. The females, daughters of the house and maid-servants, lay in rooms on one side, say the right, the maids in those most distant, reached through the apartments of the young ladies; those of the men lay on the left, the sons of the house nearest the chamber of the squire, the serving-men furthest off.

When the party in the house retired for the night, a file of damsels marched up-stairs, domestic servants first, passed through the room of their master and mistress, then through those of the young ladies, and were shut in at the end; next entered the daughters of the house to their several chambers, the youngest lying near the room of the serving-maids, the eldest most outside, near that of her father and mother. That procession disposed of, a second mounted the stairs, consisting of the men of the house, the stable-boy first, and the son and heir last, and were disposed of similarly to the females, but on the opposite side of the staircase. Then, finally, the squire and his wife retired to roost in the chamber that commanded those of all the rest of the household. This arrangement still subsists in our old fashioned farm-houses.

Now may be understood the odd provision in a will proved in the Consistory Court of Canterbury in 1652 (Bowyer, f. 57)—"I give to my son Thomas the sole fee-simple and inheritance of my dwelling-house, and all my lands and hereditaments thereto belonging, to him and to his heirs for ever. And my will is, that Joan my daughter shall have free ingress, egress, and regress to the bedd in the chambre where she now lieth, so long as she continueth unmarried."

But to this arrangement followed another, more practical and convenient, that of having a grand corridor up-stairs, out of which opened the doors of the bedrooms; or, where there was a glazed-in quadrangle with staircase and landings around it, there the doors of the bedrooms opened from these landings. The corridor was used as a room for dancing, or for music, or for games; it was the recreation place of the house on a rainy day. Being up-stairs, and away from library and parlours, the young people might skip, and play blind-man's buff, dance, and disturb no one; nor was there much furniture in these corridors to stand in the way and get knocked over.

This corridor is a feature of an old house so very dear to young folks, and so very advantageous to their health, that it is a pity in our modern houses we have got rid of it.

A word on the furniture of our old country houses must not be omitted. Unfortunately there set in at the beginning of this century a most detestable fashion in furniture, absolutely void of taste; and to make room for the villainous articles then imported into our old country houses, much beautiful old work was turned out, very often was given to servants when they married. The consequence is, that much of it passed into cottages, where it soon got destroyed. It was not only old carved oak that was cast forth, for much of that had been got rid of in the Georgian epoch, but even the beautiful polished wood cabinets, chests of drawers, and Chippendale chairs of a more recent period.

Of early furniture, I mean mediæval, little remains in our houses, for one reason, because there was in them very little. The era of furniture was begun with the Tudor monarchs; it was all of oak, and the carving was influenced much by Holbein, who inspired artists with admiration for German Renaissance. Cabinets with architectural façades and heavy oak furniture continued in the Elizabethan and Stuart periods. The date of a chair can be told approximately by the position of the rail binding together the legs. The primary object of this brace was, to hold the legs firmly, but it was also found to possess the not less important advantage of providing a person sitting in the chair with the means of keeping his feet from the cold stone-slabbed pavement. When boarded floors came into fashion, it became no longer necessary to have the front brace of the chair placed so near the floor, and to give more freedom to the feet it was gradually heightened. Some time after this the side braces were raised to the same level as the front brace, and later still, as the first necessity for their use was gradually lost sight of, they were dispensed with altogether. This was the first step towards the bad system of construction now almost universally practised, of leaving the legs of chairs without any support at their lower extremities. At the beginning of this century a still further deviation from right principles ensued. The legs of chairs were made to curve, and often to curve in such a manner as to make them unserviceable for supporting the weight reposed upon them.

"Let us examine an old oak chair, and see how it was constructed. In the first place, we shall find that the whole of the work is executed in solid oak, the uprights forming the back, and the back legs being made of one continuous piece; this at once gives strength and backbone to the whole structure. The framework holding the seat is next securely tenoned, and pinned with oaken pegs into the four legs, thus binding the whole of the parts firmly together. Even at this stage we have a far more strongly constructed

31

piece of work than the modern chair when quite completed; the old workman, however, not content with this, next turned his attention to the weakest part of all—the feet of the chair—and securely fastened them together about three or four inches from the floor with four strong braces, tenoning each brace at both ends into the legs of the chair, and securing it, as before, with oaken pegs. This last addition made the whole a perfectly strong and almost indestructible piece of framing, and constitutes one of the most essential differences in the construction of ancient and modern furniture. The legs of most modern chairs are made to depend entirely for strength on their hold, at one end, to the framing of the seat of the chair, into which they are generally only glued. The legs of the ancient chair, on the other hand, are secured at both ends; and the four braces connecting them together act as struts as well as ties; they form an admirable protection against any blow the chair may receive at its lower extremities. Many of the old chairs constructed on these excellent principles are now in good condition, after nearly two hundred years of daily use."[2]

In mediæval times there were trestles and boards for a dining-table; but in Chaucer's time fixed tables were coming into use. He tells how that in the rich and luxurious Franklin's house there were—

"Alle deyntees that men cowde thynke,

* * * * * *

His table dormant in his halle alway
Stood redy covered al the longe day."

The "table dormant" was used only by very rich people; it was a new fashion at the close of the fourteenth century, and was expensive. It took its name from the fact that it was slept upon at night; it served as a bed for one of the men who lay in the hall. This table consisted of a single long trestle with a plank on it. It had but two legs, one at each end, and a beam between supported by struts. But at the same time that these tables came into fashion, another variety was in use, supported by a pair of short trestles at each end. The top of this table was also formed of planks, but they were hinged together so as to be easily folded up and removed, when additional space was required. A table of this kind is referred to by

---

[2] Examples of Carved Oak Woodwork, by W. Bliss Sanders. London: 1883.

Shakespeare in Romeo and Juliet, when, as Capulet enters the hall with his guests, he exclaims—

> "Come, musicians, play.
> A hall! a hall! give room, and foot it, girls.
> More light, you knaves; and turn the tables up."

A remarkably cleverly constructed table of the reign of Elizabeth exists at Slade in South Devon. It is based on the plan of the table dormant, but is convertible into a settle when no longer required as a table; the planking rests on the settle arms when serving for a board, and slides back and assumes an erect position when required as a settle back.

A "drawing-table" was a third variety. It was one that was square framed, but could be drawn out at both ends, so as to nearly double its normal length.

In a paper on 'Our Household Furniture,' contributed to the Art Journal by Mr. G. T. Robinson, an illustration of one of these tables is given; and in speaking of the ingenuity displayed in the construction of the sliding leaves, he says, "The whole mechanism is admirably considered for the purpose it has to fulfil. Indeed its adaptation for its purpose was so good that the principle was long retained; and Sheraton, so late as the commencement of the present century, advocates its use for many writing or other tables, and gives the rule for finding the exact rake of the slides, and the technical details of all the other parts."

It is difficult to understand why so admirable and simple an arrangement was abandoned, for anything more clumsy and unsatisfactory than the method adopted in our modern dining-room tables for accomplishing a similar result can hardly be imagined.[3] The only modern examples I have seen are some manufactured by a firm in Brussels (Wattier, Steenpoort).

I confess that I look back with regret to the old highly polished mahogany table for dessert. The modern system of covering the table with white, and strips of coloured silk, and setting it with sprigs of ferns and flowers is very pretty, but then for the sake of this prettiness we are letting the polish of our tables go down. Hardly anywhere now does the butler care to keep up the polish of the table; he used to take a pride in it, now he knows that it is never seen. Yet I know of two or three old country houses into which the

---

[3] Mr. Bliss Saunders gives details of one of these in the work above referred to.

Russian fashion has not penetrated, and where even to this day the mahogany is shown, and shines like a mirror.

> "Hail, good comrades, every one,
> Round the polished table;
> Pass the bottle with the sun,
> Drink, sirs! whilst ye're able.
> Life is but a little span,
> Full of painful thinking;
> Let us live as fits a man,
> No good liquors blinking!"

So sang our grandfathers; but the song has gone out with the polished table, and with the polished table the quiet enjoyable drinking of good port and sherry after the retirement of the ladies. The cigarette is lighted—and who can enjoy port with the air full of its perfumes?—and no sooner is the wine begun to be appreciated, than the tray of coffee is presented, dug into the side, as a reminder that now-a-days the pleasant hour with good wine and agreeable male companions is cut down to a quarter of an hour—has gone out of fashion, along with the polished table, and we must away into the drawing-room to talk empty nothingnesses, and listen to bad music.

But we must not spend too much time over tables and chairs. Marquetry became the fashion under William and Mary, when upright clocks, bureaux, and chairs were thus decorated. Under Louis XIV. a new style of decoration was introduced by one André Charles Buhl, who gave his name to it. He was chief upholsterer to the king, and his rich and brilliant marquetry of tortoise-shell and brass, so combined as to form figures and subjects, was extensively used in the furnishing of the new palace at Versailles.

The fashion extended to England, and where tortoise-shell was not employed, the ground was gilt, then painted over with black, leaving a pattern in gold uncovered, and the whole was washed over with a reddish-brown lacquer, which gave the effect of tortoise-shell. Spaces thus treated were relieved by raised work in wood carved and gilt in relief, in representation of Buhl's brass work. We find this chiefly in mirror and picture-frames.

Then followed the reign of Louis XV., the age of rococo, of shell-shaped curves set against each other back to back. It may have been barbarous, but it was rich and beautiful. Then walls were painted white and picked out with gold, the clearest, most brilliant, turquoise-blues and rose-carmines came in. Painters devoted themselves to the decoration of panels in the walls of rooms and to ceilings, the dessus-de-portes, over-doors, generally in chiaroscuro, shepherds and shepherdesses, nymphs, cherubs. There was a certain amount of sombreness in the old Elizabethan house, in the dark oak panelling, in the olive-greens of the tapestry, that was distasteful to the merry men of the epoch from Charles II. to the first Georges, and they set themselves to make their interiors as sparkling with gold and brilliant colour as possible on a white instead of a dark ground.

The discovery of Pompeii caused a return to a simpler style of decoration, to purer forms; and marquetry furniture was manufactured in exotic woods, enriched with ormolu mountings. Paintings were executed on copper and let into chimney-pieces, of great delicacy and charm.

Chippendale, Heppelwhite, and Sheraton are names associated with the mahogany furniture of the last century, with tables with pierced galleries, chairs with open strap work backs, cabinets of graceful curves, all of admirable workmanship. Indeed cabinet-making never attained a higher degree of delicacy and perfection than at this period. I would point to some of the bureaux of this date as real marvels of workmanship. And look at the backs of the chairs—a good Chippendale chair has the upright curled back at the top, in a manner remarkable for beauty, and right in principle, for it exposes no sharp angles to suffer from a blow. The satin-wood furniture, some of it with medallions painted on it, sideboards, work-tables, chiffoniers, sometimes only decorated with delicate garlands of laurel or bay painted or inlaid on the satin-wood, is not to be disregarded. The only furniture that cannot be loved is that of the first thirty years of this century, when it violated all true principles of construction, and manifested neither invention nor taste in design.

Before leaving the consideration of old country houses, one word must be said about their setting. We now-a-days, when we build a mansion, look out for the top of a hill, a good windy, exposed spot. It never occurs to us that half the charm of a house consists in the way in which it is framed. The mediæval Germans lived on the tops of rocks, but then their houses were castles, partly for defence, and partly because they knew what was fit to be done. Artistically, they made these castles eminently picturesque with towers and gables that cut the sky. We do not now build castles, but—well, the word is suitable—boxes; and a box looks like a box on the top of a hill against the sky, and nothing can make it look other. Our English forefathers, in their sense of security, and in their love of sun and shelter, sought out a hillside, and built their mansions so as to have rising ground behind it, to back it, and where they had not a hill, there they had a wood of tall trees. A house thus set is like a picture in a frame, a pretty face in a real bonnet. I do not think that ladies who, in pursuance of a vile fashion, wear hats, can be aware of the loss of charm to the face. Let them take an ancestral portrait out of its frame, and hang it thus naked against the wall. They will see at once that the frame insulates it, draws attention to its beauties and enhances them. It is the same with a house. It may be good architecturally, but unless it be backed up by a green hill covered with wood, tall Scotch pines, the haunt of rooks, umbrageous beech, in autumn trees of gold, it is nothing but an architectural study. How naked, how forlorn a dear old house looks that has lost its timber that surrounded it! I know one or two old mansions that have been converted into farm-houses, and their rear-guard of timber hewn down and sold. There is a broken-hearted look about them that reminds one of a carriage-horse degraded to go in a cart. It feels its degradation, loses flesh, gloss, and spirit.

I was one day walking with an old friend whom fate doomed to live abroad all his life, but whose heart was ever in his native land. We were strolling near an old mansion, in its park, when he stopped, looked at it, and said, "Ye gentlemen of England, that dwell at home at ease—and in what ease! in what peace and beauty! Indeed, I think that, as in all the world there is not a type of man nobler, better, more complete in every way than the true English gentleman, so do I think that nowhere—not approachably even, anywhere—is there to be found a house like the old English country house." And in my heart I responded, Amen—It is so.

CHAPTER IV

THE OLD GARDEN

JUST before the breaking forth of the French Revolution, the Abbé de Lille composed a poem in four cantos, entitled Les Jardins, in which he enthusiastically urged the abandonment of all formality in the laying out of a garden, and the adoption of the new English style of irregularity.

> "Avant de planter, avant que du terrain
> Votre béche imprudente entame le sein,
> Pour donnez aux jardins une forme plus pure,
> Observez, connoissez, imitez la nature."

An agreeable wildness—that was what was to be sought. The Revolution came in, and hacked the gardens about, and reduced them all to the state of wildness.

What the Abbé de Lille wrote against was the artificiality of the garden arrangement that had been in vogue till then. Horace Walpole had already written in the same strain. A rage had set in in England for remodelling the gardens, and the new fashion was called "English gardening."

Pliny the younger, in his delightful letters, speaks of his gardens. As his Laurentine villa was his winter retreat, it is not surprising that the gardens there take no prominent part of his account. All he says of them is, that the gestatio, or exercise ground, surrounded the garden, and was bounded by a box-hedge; where the box had perished, there were planted tufts of rosemary. He mentions his vine-walk and his trees, mostly mulberry and fig, as the soil was unsuited for other trees. On his Tuscan villa he is more diffuse; the garden takes up a good part of the description. He tells of the strange shapes into which his box-trees were clipped, his slopes, his terraces, shrubs methodically trimmed, a marble basin, fountain, a cascade, bay-trees alternating with plane-trees, a long straight walk, from which branched off others hedged by apple-trees in espalier, and by box, and ornamented with obelisks. Something like a rural view was, indeed, contrived amidst so much artificiality, but was speedily forgotten amidst the stiff lines of box and the trimmed cypresses.

In the paintings of Herculaneum we see the representations of gardens; they are square enclosures, formed by trellis-work and espaliers, and regularly ornamented with vases, fountains, and statues, elegantly symmetrical. Now this arrangement of a garden continued in Italy. It never changed, and the villa gardens in and about Rome to this day reproduce the plans and character of those that flourished there in the classic age.

The villa-gardens in and about Rome! I cannot write the words without an ache of heart, for I know that they are disappearing rapidly, inevitably. Along the Via Salaria I saw three in process of destruction during the late winter and spring of 1889. A great slice of the Borghese grounds is being devastated to make room for hideous streets and squares. The Wolkonski gardens have been curtailed; those of Villa Massimo Arsoli adjoining, almost destroyed and built over; the Rospigliosi gardens gone; others doomed; the glorious Ludovisi gardens, with their cypresses and ilexes towering above the closed Porta Pinciana and the ancient boundary wall, are in process of extermination. "The grounds, which were of an extent extraordinary when considered as being within the walls of a capital, were laid out by Le Nôtre, and were in the stiff French style of high-clipped hedges, and avenues adorned with vases and sarcophagi. With the fury against trees which characterizes Italians, all the magnificent ilexes and cypresses were cut down as soon as the land was secured, and the plots of building-land rendered altogether hideous and undesirable. In a few years not a trace will remain of the picturesque glories of this once noble villa, which, if acquired by the municipality, who refused to purchase it, might have been made into public gardens of beauty unrivalled in any European capital."[4]

The railway station, with its sheds and sidings, occupies the once matchless gardens of the Villa Massimo Negroni, celebrated for its exquisite cypress avenues and its stately terrace, lined with ancient orange-trees and noble sarcophagi. The ground was confiscated by the State, and the destruction of this fair scene broke the heart of the owner, Prince Massimo. The sweet gardens of the Villa Strozzi are gone, now built over with ugly houses. Outside the Porta Pia grand old gardens are being devastated also.

The Medici gardens remain; Hawthorn thus described them. "They are laid out in the old fashion of straight paths, with borders of box, which form hedges of great height and density, and are shorn and trimmed to the evenness of a wall of stone at the top and sides. There are green alleys, with long vistas, overshadowed by ilex-trees; and at each intersection of the paths the visitor finds seats of

---

[4] Hare, Walks in Rome.

lichen-covered stone to repose on, and marble statues that look forlornly at him, regretful of their lost noses. In the more open portions of the gardens, before the sculptured front of the villa, you see fountains and flower-beds; and, in their season, a profusion of roses, from which the genial sun of Italy distils a fragrance to be scattered abroad by the no less genial breeze."

The Boboli gardens at Florence remain to testify to the ancient arrangement, with high walls of evergreens and long avenues hedged up ten or twelve feet, dense and impervious, above which rise the spires of cypress and the domes of the stone-pine.

Our English gardens were modelled on those of the Italian palaces, the same subdivision of squares into sections, with trimmed box enclosing them, and with a statue or a fountain, or a carved and shaped yew in the midst. The gardens were invariably enclosed within walls. Where the ground sloped, at great expense it was shaped into terraces, reached by flights of steps. The greatest exactness in the design was aimed at. As Pope observed—

> "Each alley has a brother,
> And half the garden just reflects the other."

When Pamela endured her persecution she was allowed to walk in the garden, but this was so walled round that escape from it was impossible. There were seats in it on which she might repose in the sun. There was a fish-pond in which she might angle, but there was only one garden-door by which egress could be obtained, and that was locked. It was the same with Clarissa Harlowe. The garden of her father's house was walled round.

The pleached alleys were constructed of lime or beech trees platted and trimmed so as to form walls of green. They were over-arched, and those walking in them were as in a green bower. I know an old château on the Moselle with such a berceau, it has in it windows commanding beautiful reaches of the river; otherwise it is completely enclosed by leaves, and fresh and sweet it is as a walk on a hot day. In England we required shade less than shelter, and the green funnels were not in such request as the long lines of lofty yew or box hedge.

In King's Views of the Seats of our Nobility and Gentry, at the beginning of the eighteenth century, we see the utmost formality. Every house is approached by two or three gardens, consisting perhaps of a gravel-walk and two grass-plats, or borders of flowers. Each rises above the other by two or three steps, and as many walls and terraces, and so many iron gates.

Sir William Temple gives us his view of what constituted a perfect garden in his day. "The perfectest figure of a garden I ever saw, either at home or abroad, was that of Moor Park, in Hertfordshire. I will describe it for a model to those that meet with such a situation, and are above the regards of common expense. It lies on the side of a hill, upon which the house stands, but not very steep. The length of the house, where the best rooms and of most use or pleasure are, lies upon the breadth of the garden; the great parlour opens into the midst of a terrace gravel-walk that lies even with it, and which may lie about three hundred paces long, and broad in proportion; the border set with standard laurels and at large distances, which have the beauty of orange-trees out of flower and fruit. From this walk are three descents by many stone steps, in the middle and at each end, into a very large parterre. This is divided into quarters by gravel-walks, and adorned with two fountains and eight statues, at the several quarters. At the end of the terrace-walk are two summer-houses, and the sides of the parterre are ranged with two large cloisters open to the garden; over these two cloisters are two terraces covered with lead and fenced with balusters; and the passage into these airy walks is out of the two summer-houses at the end of the first terrace-walk. The cloister facing the south is covered with vines. From the middle of the parterre is a descent by many steps into the lower garden, which is all fruit-trees, ranged about the several quarters of a wilderness, which is very shady; the walks here are all green, and there is a grotto embellished with figures of shell rock-work, fountains, and water-works."

Nothing could be more formal, and nothing, I think, could be more charming. Why should we imitate wild nature? The garden is a product of civilization. Why any more make of our gardens imitation wild nature, than paint our children with woad, and make them run about naked in an effort to imitate nature unadorned? The very charm of a garden is that it is taken out of savagery, trimmed, clothed, and disciplined. The wall and hedge are almost necessaries with us, to cut off the wind. See how flowers of all kinds luxuriate, if given the screen from the biting blast! If they like it, why should not we?

I allow that the hacking of trees into fantastical shapes deserved the scourge administered in the one hundred and seventy-third number of The Guardian, Sept. 29th, 1713. The writer there says—"How contrary to simplicity is the modern practice of gardening; we seem to make it our study to recede from nature, not only in the various tonsure of greens into the most regular and formal shapes, but even in monstrous attempts beyond the reach of the art itself; we run into sculpture, and are yet better pleased to have our trees in the most awkward figures of men and animals, than in the most regular of their own. A citizen is no sooner proprietor of a couple of yews, but he entertains thoughts of erecting them into giants, like those of Guildhall. I know an eminent cook, who beautified his country-seat with a coronation dinner in greens, where you see the champion flourishing on horseback at one end of the table, and the queen in perpetual youth at the other.

"For the benefit of all my loving countrymen of this curious taste, I shall here publish a catalogue of greens to be disposed of by an eminent town gardener, who has lately applied to me upon this head. My correspondent is arrived at such perfection, that he cuts family pieces of men, women, or children. Any ladies that please may have their own effigies in myrtle, or their husbands in horn-beam. I shall proceed to his catalogue, as he sent it for my recommendation.

"'Adam and Eve in yew; Adam a little shattered by the fall of the tree of knowledge in the great storm, Eve and the serpent very flourishing.

"'The Tower of Babel, not yet finished.

"'St. George in box; his arm scarce long enough, but will be in condition to strike the dragon by next April.

"'A Queen Elizabeth in phylyræa, a little inclining to the green-sickness, but of full growth.

"'An old maid-of-honour in worm-wood.

"'Divers eminent poets in bays, somewhat blighted, to be disposed of a pennyworth.

"'A quickset hog shot up into a porcupine, by its being forgot a week in rainy weather,' &c."

But these absurdities do not affect the question of hedges. I know a hedge of clay and stone built up eight feet, and above that crowned with holly and thorn, running from east to west, but with a point or two of west in its face. I remember an old man, a rector, chronically affected with bronchitis for fifteen years, who felt the solace of this charming hedge through the whole time. He could crawl out there when the sun shone, and disregard the north and east winds. In that hedge the primrose and the foxglove were out prematurely. The rabbits loved it dearly, and made it untidy with their burrowings in the warm dry clay under the roots of the bushes.

If a ruthless craving for vistas had not prevailed in and after Horace Walpole's time, every one of our country houses and parsonages would have had these sweet sheltered walks, where invalids could creep along and bask in the sun. We have had them demolished, and so must away to the Riviera. Evelyn had a great holly hedge in his garden at Sayes Court, four hundred feet in length, five feet in diameter, and nine feet high; and when the Court was let to the Czar Peter, during his visit to the Deptford dockyard, that barbarian drove his wheel-barrow through it, and so injured the hedge that Evelyn claimed damages, and received one hundred and fifty pounds in compensation.

Another charming feature of the old garden—and one that was costly to execute—was the terrace. The slope of the hillside was taken in hand and was cut away, so as to produce a level lawn with a level, horizontal terrace-walk above it, and perhaps, where the slope admitted of it, a second and superior terrace. These terrace walls gave shelter, and as walks were always dry, the drainage from them being rapid. Trees, shrubs, flowers planted on them throve; there was no stagnation of water about their roots, and the sun, striking against the wall that enclosed the earth for their roots, made it warm, cherishing to the plants, as a hot bottle is a comfort to you who suffer from cold feet in your bed.

Nowhere have I seen roses so revel, go mad with delight and gratitude as in these terrace gardens. The rose is peculiarly averse to wet feet. See how the wild rose thrives in the clay-banked-up hedge!—a hedge that seems to have no moisture in it, the earth of which crumbles between the finger and thumb like snuff.

Then, again, the rose hates wind, and the terrace wall serves as a screen to it against its enemy. And—for human roses!

Last summer I attended a garden-party at an ancient country house with an old-fashioned garden. From the lawn in front of the porch a flight of granite steps led to a terrace nine feet above the lawn. This terrace was planted with venerable yew-trees, under which were little tables spread with fruit and cool drinks, and cakes. A second flight of steps gave access to a second terrace some twelve or fourteen feet higher, planted with flowers, and backed to the north by a lofty garden wall.

I do not think that, off the stage, I have seen any effect more beautiful than that of the young girls in their bright and many-tinted summer dresses, flitting about; some under the shade of the yews on terrace number one, some looking at the flowers a stage higher, on terrace number two, and some ascending and others descending the broad flight of steps that led to these terraces, like the angels in Jacob's vision.

The walls supporting the terraces served another purpose than that of sustaining the roots of trees and flowers on the stages;

as rain fell on the terraces, it exuded between the joints of the stones and nourished a fairy world of lichen, moss, and ferns. This was the wall shaded by the yews. The other was hugged and laughed over by roses, honeysuckle, and wisteria.

We have got almost no gardens left in England in their primitive condition, only the wreckage of their beauty. But, as the old woman said who sniffed the empty amphora of old Falernian wine, "If what remains be so good, what must you have been when full!"

Now let us see what Horace Walpole tells us of the devastation of these beautiful old gardens. "No succeeding generation," he says, "in an opulent and luxurious country contents itself with the perfection established by its ancestors; more perfect perfection was still sought, and improvements had gone on, till London and Wise had stocked all our gardens with giants, animals, monsters, coats of arms and mottoes, in yew, box, and holly. Bridgman, the next fashionable designer of gardens, was far more chaste—he banished verdant sculpture, and did not even revert to the square precision of the foregoing age. He enlarged his plans, disdained to make every division tally to its opposite, and though he still adhered much to straight walks with high-clipped hedges, they were only his great lines; the rest he diversified by wilderness, and with loose groves of oak, though still within surrounding hedges. As his reformation gained footing, he ventured to introduce cultivated fields and even morsels of forest appearance, by the sides of those endless and tiresome walks.

"But the capital stroke, the leading step to all that has followed,"—I shiver as I write these words,—"was the destruction of walls for boundaries, and the invention of fosses—an attempt then deemed so astonishing, that the common people called them Ha! Ha's! to express their surprise at finding a sudden and unperceived check to their walk. No sooner was this simple enchantment made, than levelling, mowing, and rolling followed. The contiguous ground of the park without the sunk fence was to be harmonized with the lawn within; and the garden in its turn was to be set free from its prim regularity, that it might assort with the wilder country without. At that moment appeared Kent, painter enough to taste the charms of landscape, bold and opinionative enough to dare and to dictate, and born with a genius to strike out a great system from the twilight of imperfect essays."

The man Kent deserved the gallows much more than many who have been hung. No one who pretended to be in fashion dared to maintain a hedge or a wall. Down went the walls, and the beautiful roses bent their heads and died; the great yew hedges were stubbed up, and the delicate children and feeble old gentlemen who had basked under the lea, also, like the roses, stooped to earth and died. All the shelter, sweetness, sun, restfulness went away. These hedges had taken a century and more to grow, they were levelled without compunction, never perhaps again to reappear.[5]

No doubt there was folly in our forefathers in trimming yews into fantastical shapes; but Kent and his followers were as extravagant in their way. Kent actually planted dead trees in lawns and parks, to give a greater air of reality to the scene. Where he was allowed he cut down, or mutilated avenues, because unnatural; but just as unnatural were his absurd vistas, dug through woods so that the eye might reach a pagoda, an obelisk, or a temple at the end.

A traveller in France in 1788, on the eve of the Revolution, gives an account of the garden of Ermenonville, laid out by M. de Girardin on the English system. "He has succeeded better in closely imitating the steps of nature than any spot I have ever seen; nothing seems laboured, nothing artificial. The ground is irregular, and the ornaments rude, though the latter approach to too great an excess. I can see no reason, if ornaments are to be made use of in such places as these (which in itself is a deviation from nature), why they should not be handsome. To see a miserable obelisk built of brick, and resembling more a chimney than a monument, is carrying the refinement of wildness to too high a pitch. If they are designed to be rude and natural, they may at the same time be grotesque and elegant. Winding along a lovely walk, through the bosom of a young wood, a gentle stream meandering by its side, we reached a charming and retired spot. A large space here opens, shaded by the thick branches of the trees, which just leave room for a softened light to insinuate itself, and for the zephyrs to breathe through; over interrupting rocks and heaps of pebbles, the water dashes along with a noise grateful and composing. Here an altar is erected, sacred to Reverie; on a rock that overhangs the stream are inscribed some pleasing lines. Hence through a varied and highly pleasing path we continued our route along the grove, meeting with different inscriptions. From thence we ascended the forest, and traversing a path rugged and grotesque, were presented with many interesting and pleasing views. Arriving on the plain, in the bosom of a wood,

---

[5] Having got rid of the wall, and finding that flowers now suffer from the wind, gardeners are fond of sinking beds, and not a few gardens are thus furnished.

we reached an extended area, in the midst of which stood a large oak, and at the end an edifice."[6]

I had written thus far, when last night there came to see me an old village singer of nigh on eighty years, always to me a welcome guest. I seated him by the fireside on a settle, and we fell to talking about gardens, when he said, "I reckon, your honour, I know a rare old-fashioned song about flowers and gardings, and them like. If your honour 'ud plase to hear me, I'll zing 'n."

Then he struck up the following quaint ballad, to an air certainly two hundred years old—

"IN A GARDEN SWEET"

Arranged by F. W. Bussell, Esq., M.A.

Two lovers in a garden sweet
Were walking side by side,
I heard how he the maid addressed,
I heard how she replied.
The garden it was very great,
With box trees in a row;
And up and down the gravell'd walk
These lovers fond did go.

"Said he, 'I prithee fix the day
Whereon we shall be wed.'
Said she, 'Thou hast a wanton mind,
I like thee not,' she said.
'For now you look at brown Nancy,
And dark eyes pleasure you;
But next declare you like the fair
Julian with eyes of blue.'

"'O pretty maid, in garden sweet,
Are flowers in each parterre,
I turn and gaze with fond amaze
At all—for all are fair.
But one I find—best to my mind,
Of all I choose but one;
I stoop and gather that choice flower,
And wear that flower alone.'"

---

[6] A Reflective Tour through Part of France. London: 1789.

45

CHAPTER V

THE COUNTRY PARSON

OF NO class of men can it be more truly said that the good they do dies with them, and that the evil lives—in the memory of men—than the country parson. Of the thousands of old rectors and vicars of past generations, how they have all slipped out of the memory of men, have left no tradition whatever behind them, if they were good! but the few bad ones did so impress themselves on their generation, that the stories of their misconduct have been handed on, and are not forgotten in a century.

In the floor of my own parish church, in the chancel, is a tombstone to a former incumbent. The name and the date have been ground away by the heels of the school-children who sit over it, but thus much of the inscription remains—

> "... The Psalmists man of yeares hee lived a score,
> Tended his flocke allone; theire ofspring did restore
> By Water into life of Grace; at font and grave,
> He served God devout: and strivd men's soules to save.
> He fedd the poore, lov'd all, and did by Pattern showe,
> As pastor to his Flocke, ye way that they shoulde go."

Not less effaced than the name is all tradition of the man whose monument proclaims his virtues. Now, I take it, for this very reason the tombstone bears true testimony. If it had told lies, every one would have known about it, and related this fact to their children; would have told anecdotes of the parson who was so unworthy, but concerning whose virtues his stone made such boast. That our old country parsons were not, as a rule, a disreputable, drinking, neglectful set of men I believe, because so few traditions of their misconduct remain.

There was a clever, pleasant book published at the beginning of this century, entitled, The Velvet Cushion. It was written by the Rev. J. W. Cunningham, Vicar of Harrow. The seventh edition, from which I quote, appeared in 1815. This book professes to tell the experiences of a pulpit cushion from pre-Reformation days to the beginning of the nineteenth century. Here is what the Cushion says—"Sir, you will be anxious, I am sure, to hear the history of some of your predecessors in the living; and it is my intention to gratify you. I think it right, however, to observe, that of a large proportion of them no very interesting records remain. Mankind are much alike, and a little country village is not likely to call out their peculiarities. Some few were mere profligates, whose memory I do not wish to perpetuate."—But it is precisely these, and only these, that the less charitable memory of man does perpetuate.—"Many of them were persons of decent, cold, correct manners, varying slightly, perhaps, in the measure of their zeal, their doctrinal exactness, their benevolence, their industry, their talents—but, in general, of that neutral class which rarely affords materials for history, or subjects of instruction. They were men of that species who are too apt to spring up in the bosom of old and prosperous establishments, whose highest praise is, that they do no harm."

No one can accuse this description as being coloured too high. It is, if I may judge by early recollections, applicable to those who occupied the parsonages twenty and thirty years later.

In my own parish in which I was reared, Romaine, one of the most brilliant luminaries of the evangelical revival, acted as curate for a while, but not the smallest trace of any tradition of his goodness, his eloquence, his zeal did I discover among the villagers. At the very time that Romaine was in this parish, there was a curate in an adjoining one who was over-fond of the bottle, and was picked up out of the ditch on more than one occasion. Neither his name nor his delinquencies are forgotten to this day.

I take it that the state in which the parish registers have been kept are a fair test as to what sort of parsons there were. Now certainly they were very neglectfully kept at the Restoration and for a short while afterwards. That is not to be wondered at. During the Commonwealth they had been taken from the parsons and committed to lay-registrars in the several parishes, who certainly kept them badly, and at the Restoration they were not at once and always reclaimed, but continued to be kept by the clerk, who stepped into the place of the registrar appointed by the Commonwealth. But in the much-maligned Hanoverian period they were carefully kept by the clergy, and as a rule neatly entered. If such an indication be worth anything, it shows that the country parsons did take pains to discharge at least one of their duties. He that is faithful in a small matter, is faithful also, we may conclude, in that which is great.

I presume that Dr. Syntax may be regarded as typical of the class, and Combe says of him—

"Of Church-preferment he had none;
Nay, all his hope of that was gone:

47

He felt that he content must be
With drudging in a curacy.
Indeed, on ev'ry Sabbath-day,
Through eight long miles he took his way,
To preach, to grumble, and to pray;
To cheer the good, to warn the sinner,
And, if he got it,—eat a dinner:
To bury these, to christen those,
And marry such fond folks as chose
To change the tenor of their life,
And risk the matrimonial strife.
Thus were his weekly journeys made,
'Neath summer suns and wintry shade;
And all his gains, it did appear,
Were only thirty pounds a-year."

And when he dies—

"The village wept, the hamlets round
Crowded the consecrated ground;
And waited there to see the end
Of Pastor, Teacher, Father, Friend."

What a charming picture does Fielding draw in his Joseph Andrews of Mr. Abraham Adams, the parson—gentle, guileless, learned, and very poor. And Goldsmith's Vicar of Wakefield—was ever a purer, sweeter type of man delineated? The description given of his parsonage and mode of life is valuable, and must be quoted; for it shows what a change has come over the parsonage and the parson's manner of intercourse with his parishioners since Goldsmith's time.

"Our little habitation was situated at the foot of a sloping hill, sheltered with a beautiful underwood behind, and prattling river before; on one side a meadow, on the other a green. My farm consisted of about twenty acres of excellent land, having given an hundred pounds for my predecessor's good-will.... My house consisted of but one story, and was covered with thatch, which gave it an air of great snugness; the walls on the inside were nicely whitewashed, and my daughters undertook to adorn them with pictures of their own designing. Though the same room served us for parlour and kitchen, that only made it warmer. Besides, as it was kept with the utmost neatness, the dishes, plates, and coppers being well scoured, and all disposed in bright rows on the shelves, the eye was agreeably relieved, and did not want richer furniture. There were three other apartments—one for my wife and me, another for our two daughters, within our own, and the third, with two beds for the rest of the children."

Our old parsonage houses precisely resembled this description, but hardly any remain. They have given way for more pretentious houses; and with the grander houses the habits and requirements of the parsons have grown.

"Nor were we without guests; sometimes Farmer Flamborough, and often the blind piper, would pay us a visit, and taste our gooseberry wine. These harmless people had several ways of being good company; for while one played, the other would sing some soothing ballad—Johnny Armstrong's Last Good Night, or The Cruelty of Barbara Allen."

Crabbe, himself a clergyman, does not give the most favourable sketch of the village parsons; and yet his country vicar is a man of perfect blamelessness.

> "Our Priest was cheerful, and in season gay;
> His frequent visits seldom fail'd to please;
> Easy himself, he sought his neighbour's ease.

> * * * * * *

> Simple he was, and loved the simple truth,
> Yet had some useful cunning from his youth;
> A cunning never to dishonour lent,
> And rather for defence than conquest meant;
> 'Twas fear of power, with some desire to rise,
> But not enough to make him enemies;
> He ever aim'd to please; and to offend
> Was ever cautious; for he sought a friend.
> Fiddling and fishing were his arts: at times
> He alter'd sermons, and he aim'd at rhymes;
> And his fair friends, not yet intent on cards,
> Oft he amused with riddles and charades.
> Mild were his doctrines, and not one discourse
> But gain'd in softness what it lost in force:
> Kind his opinions; he would not receive
> An ill report, nor evil act believe.

> * * * * * *

> Though mild benevolence our Priest possess'd,

'Twas but by wishes or by words expressed.
Circles in water, as they wider flow,
The less conspicuous in their progress grow,
And when, at last, they touch upon the shore,
Distinction ceases, and they're viewed no more.
His love, like the last circle, all embraced,
But with effect that never could be traced.
Now rests our Vicar.—They who knew him best
Proclaim his life t' have been entirely—rest.
The rich approved,—of them in awe he stood;
The poor admired,—they all believed him good;
The old and serious of his habits spoke;
The frank and youthful loved his pleasant joke;
Mothers approved a safe contented guest,
And daughters one who backed each small request;
In him his flock found nothing to condemn;
Him sectaries liked,—he never troubled them:
No trifles fail'd his yielding mind to please,
And all his passions sunk in early ease;
Nor one so old has left this world of sin,
More like the being that he entered in."

Clever, true, and cutting. Crabbe knew the class, its excellences and its weaknesses. We are considering the excellences now; we will recur to the weaknesses later.

Fielding does, in his Joseph Andrews, give us a study of another type of parson—Trulliber, "whom Adams found stript into his waistcoat, with an apron on, and a pail in his hands, just come from serving his hogs; for Mr. Trulliber was a parson on Sundays, but all the other six might be more properly called a farmer. He occupied a small piece of land of his own, besides which he rented a considerable deal more. His wife milked his cows, managed his dairy, and followed the market with butter and eggs. The hogs fell chiefly to his care, which he carefully waited on at home, and attended to fairs; on which occasion he was liable to many jokes, his own size being with much ale rendered little inferior to that of the beasts he sold.... His voice was loud and hoarse, and his accent extremely broad. To complete the whole, he had a stateliness in his gait when he walked, not unlike of a goose, only he stalked slower."

But this parson was only a boor, he was not disorderly.

I have an old coachman, near eighty, who has been in the family since he was a boy, and of whom I get many stories of how the world went at the beginning of this century. Said he to me one

50

day, "My old uncle he lived in Maristowe; he was bedridden nigh on twenty years, and in all those years Parson Teasdale didn't miss coming to see and read and pray with him every day, Sunday and week-day alike."

We make much fuss about parochial visiting now, but is there any visiting like that? In The Velvet Cushion, a dialogue between the Vicar and his wife is chronicled.

"'I am not sure,' said the Vicar, 'that it is not a presumptuous reliance upon the goodness of God,—an abuse of the doctrine of Divine mercy, that has kept me at home to-day, when I should have gone to visit old Dame Wilkins. An' so now, my dear, let us go to Mary Wilkins' directly.' Her bonnet was soon on, and they hobbled down the village almost as fast as if their house had been on fire. Mary Wilkins was a poor good woman, to whom the Vicar's visit three times a week had become almost one of the necessaries of life. It was now two hours beyond the time he usually came; and had she been awake, she would really have been pained by the delay. But, happily, she had fallen into a profound sleep, and when he put his foot on the threshold, and in his old-fashioned way said, 'Peace be with you,' she was just awaking. This comforted our good man, and, as he well knew where all comfort comes from, he thanked God in his heart even for this."

The old parsons lived more on the social level of the farmers and yeomen than of the squires, but they were in many cases men of very considerable culture. It was not, however, those who were the best scholars who were the best parsons. I will give presently my reminiscences of one of the last of the old scholar-parsons. Unfortunately, scholarship is on the decline, at all events among those who occupy country parsonages.

It has been often charged against the old parsons, that they preached mere morality, and above the heads of their people, interlarding their sermons with quotations in Greek and Latin. As for preaching morality—I do not care to apologize for their doing that. Nothing better can be preached; nothing was more necessary to be preached in the last century. Judging by the registers of baptisms in parishes, at no time was there so much immorality among village people than at that period when our country parsons were charged with preaching morality—excepting always the present. Those who made this a matter of accusation, meant that the Gospel, as they called their peculiar view of religion, was not insisted on; forgetting all the while that the Gospel is pretty well stuffed with exhortations to morality, and above all, that model for all sermons, the one preached on the Mount. But I do not believe

51

that mere morality, apart from Christian faith, was preached. There is a pretty passage in The Velvet Cushion descriptive of a sermon at the beginning of this century, which I cannot take to be a description of something quite extraordinary and out of the way.

"'My love,' said the Vicar, 'this fact is worth a thousand arguments—the common people heard Christ gladly. Socinianism never fails to drive them away. A religion without a Saviour is the temple without the Shechinah, and its worshippers will all desert it. Few men in the world have less pretensions as a preacher than myself,—my voice, my look, my manner, all of a very ordinary nature,—and yet, I thank God, there is scarcely a corner of our little church where you might not find a streaming eye or a beating heart. The reason is—that I speak of Christ; and if there is not a charm in the word, there is the train of fears, and hopes, and joys which it carries along with it. The people feel, and then they must listen.'"

Evelyn in his Diary says, in 1683, "A stranger, and old man, preached—much after Bishop Andrews' method, full of logical divisions, in short and broken periods, and Latin sentences, now quite out of fashion in the pulpit, which is grown into a far more profitable way of plain and practical discourses, of which sort this nation, or any other, never had greater plenty or more profitable, I am confident."

Pepys is hardly to be quoted as a judge, as he went to church to see pretty faces, not, or not mainly, to hear sermons, and his criticism is not always to be trusted.

"1667, 26th May, the Lord's Day. I went by water to Westminster to the parish church, and there did entertain myself with my perspective glass up and down the church, by which I had the great pleasure of seeing and gazing at a great many very fine women; and what with that, and sleeping, I passed away the time till the sermon was done."

"1667, 20th August. Turned into St. Dunstan's church, where I heard an able sermon of the minister of the place; and stood by a pretty, modest maid, whom I did labour to take by the hand; but she would not, but got further and further from me; and at last I could perceive her to take pins out of her pocket to prick me if I should touch her again,—which seeing, I did forbear, and was glad I did spy her design. And then I fell to gaze upon another pretty maid in a pew close to me, and she on me; and I did go about to take her by the hand, which she suffered a little, and then withdrew. So the sermon ended, and the church broke up, and my amours ended also."

"1667, 25th August, Lord's Day. Up and to church, thinking to see Betty Michell, and did stay an hour in the crowd, thinking, by the end of a nose that I saw, that it had been her; but at last the head turned towards me, and it was her mother, which vexed me. So I back to my boat."

No, Pepys was no judge of a good sermon, his mind was otherwise engaged.

Sermons now-a-days produce little or no effect, because there are too many of them. The ears of hearers have been tickled till they are no longer capable of sensation. One hears curates boast of having preached some seven sermons in one week, and miserable stuff it must have been that flowed so freely; and yet good enough for the hearers, who, by accustoming their ears to be always hearing, are unable to appreciate a really good discourse, or if they appreciate, allow it to produce no effect whatever upon them. Our audiences in church are like those who live in railway arches, who become so accustomed to the rush overhead of trains, that none ever rouse them, and they cannot sleep without the intermittent rush to lull them.

The sermons of the end of last century and the beginning of this do not please us, because they are cast in a different mould, they generally appeal to a different side of us than do those of the present day. They were addressed to the natural, healthy conscience, and to plain, everyday common-sense, such as all men possess. Modern sermons are appeals to the feelings, amiable, sentimental emotions, and these amiable, sentimental emotions have become accustomed to be scratched, like cats, and purr when that is done. It was an epithet of scorn launched on Pope Damasus, that he was "ear-scratcher" to the ladies,—such is, however, the highest glory of a modern preacher.

Crabbe undoubtedly hit the old country parsons on their weak point when he said of his vicar, that his main characteristic was timidity. He was infinitely blameless, but also immeasurably afraid.

> "Thus he his race began, and to the end
> His constant care was, no man to offend;
> No haughty virtues stirr'd his peaceful mind;
> Nor urged the Priest to leave the Flock behind;
> He was his Master's soldier, but not one
> To lead an army of His martyrs on:
> Fear was his ruling passion."

Courage is born of conviction, and our old English country parsons had no definite convictions, a sort of vague, nebulous, inchoate notion that Christianity was all right, and that the Church of England was a via media, and they deprecated anything like giving precision and outline to faith, and assuming a direct walk which was not a perpetual dodging between opposed errors. I ventured in one of my novels, Red-Spider, to sketch this sort of parson, who never in the pulpit insisted on a doctrine lest he should offend a Dissenter, nor on a duty lest he should make a Churchman uneasy. And it was characteristic of the race. In the Faroes there are sixteen different names for fogs, and the articles of the Christian faith were only varieties in fogs to these spiritual pastors. The nebulous theory prevailed in astronomy, and in divinity as well. Some old-fashioned people resented the resolution of the nebulæ into fixed stars; and so also in that other province do they look on it as next to sacrilege to give to faith definition.

It is, however, only since parsons have begun to see definite ends that they have assumed any steadfastness in their walk and directness in their course. In Fielding's time the country parsons wore their cassocks as a usual dress. "Adams stood up," he relates, "and presented a figure to the gentleman which would have moved laughter in many, for his cassock had just fallen down below his great-coat, that is to say, it reached his knees, whereas the skirts of his great-coat descended no lower than half-way down his thighs."

The bands were always worn, the makeshift for the old Steenkirk tie of fine white linen edged with more or less deep lace. Knee-breeches, buckled shoes, and a black cocked hat completed his attire.

Some of the old Derby Uncle Toby jugs represent the beer-drinking parson of an age a little later. The cassock has disappeared, and he wears a clerical long black coat, with bands and white stockings. The apron of the bishop is the reminiscence of the cassock, as the hat tied up with strings of the archdeacon is the last survival of the cocked hat.

The parson and his parishioners were on very good terms. When the Vicar of Wakefield came to his new cure, the village turned out to meet him with pipe and drum. Nevertheless there was occasional friction, mainly, if not altogether, relative to tithe gathering. There is a harvest-home song Dryden wrote for, or introduced into his play, King Arthur; or, The British Worthy, in 1691, which forms part of the enchantments of Merlin, and is sung by Comus and a set of peasants—

"We have cheated the parson, we'll cheat him again,
For why should a blockhead have one in ten?

One in ten,
One in ten;
For why should a blockhead have one in ten,
For prating so long, like a book-learned sot,
Till pudding and dumpling burn to pot?
Burn to pot."

There can be little question that the parson did get cheated over and over again, and bore it without a murmur.

An amusing ballad is sung to this day in the west of England relative to the way in which parsons were treated by their parishioners—

"There wor a man in our town,
I knowed him well, 'twor Passon Brown,
A man of credit and renown,
For—he wor our Passon.

Passon he had got a sheep,
Merry Christmas he would keep;
Decent Passon he—and cheap,
Well-spoke—and not a cross 'un.

Us had gotten nort to eat,
So us stole the Passon's sheep—
Merry Christmas us would keep;
We ate 'n for our dinner.

Us enjoyed our Christmas day;
Passon preached, and said, 'Let's pray,
But I'm a fasting saint; aye, aye!
You'm each a wicked sinner.'

Cruel vex'd wor Passon Brown,
Sick to death he laid him down
Passonless was soon our town,
For why?—we'd starved our Passon.

Tell'y—did'y ever hear
Such a story, true but queer,
How 'twixt Christmas and New Year
The flock had ate their Passon?"

There was non-residence undoubtedly previous to the Act against holding more than one living at a time, unless near together. Men of birth and influence obtained a good deal of preferment, but never in post-Reformation times to the extent that this abuse existed before. To take but one instance. Thomas Cantilupe, who died in 1282, was Precentor and Canon of York, Archdeacon of Stafford and Canon of Lichfield, Canon of London, Canon of Hereford, and held the livings of Doderholt, Hampton, Aston, Wintringham, Deighton, Rippel, Sunterfield, and apparently also Prestbury. Pretty well! It was never so bad in the maligned Hanoverian period.

I had a living in Essex which was held formerly by a certain Bramston Staynes, who was a squarson in Essex, and held simultaneously three other livings; there was one curate to serve the three churches. The rector is said to have visited one of his livings twice only in the twenty years of his incumbency—once to read himself in, the other time to settle some dispute relative to the payment of his tithes.

I can recall several instances of the old scholar-parson, a man chap-ful of quotations. One, a very able classic, and a great naturalist, was rather fond of the bottle. "Mr. West," said a neighbour one day, "I hear you have a wonderfully beautiful spring of water in your glebe." "Beautiful! surpassing! fons Blandusiæ, splendidior vitro!— water so good that I never touch it—afraid of drinking too much of it."

Some twenty-five years ago I knew another, a fine scholar, an old bachelor, living in a very large rectory. He was a man of good presence, courteous, old-world manners, and something of old-world infirmities. His sense of his religious responsibilities in the parish was different in quality to that affected now-a-days.

He was very old when I knew him, and was often laid up with gout. One day, hearing that he was thus crippled, I paid him a visit, and encountered a party of women descending the staircase from his room. When I entered he said to me, "I suppose you met little Mary So-and-so and Janie What's-her-name going out? I've been churching them up here in my bed-room, as I can't go to church."

When a labourer desired to have his child privately baptized, he provided a bottle of rum, a pack of cards, a lemon, and a basin of pure water, then sent for the parson and the farmer for whom he worked. The religious rite over, the basin was removed, the table cleared, cards and rum produced, and sat down to. On such occasions the rector did not return home till late, and the housekeeper left the library window unhasped for the master, but locked the house doors. Under the library window was a violet bed, and it was commonly reported that the rector had on more than one occasion slept in that bed after a christening. Unable to heave up his big body to the sill of the window, he had fallen back among the violets, and there slept off the exertion.

I never had the opportunity of hearing the old fellow preach. His conversation—whether addressing a gentleman, a lady, or one of the lower classes—was garnished with quotations from the classic authors, Greek and Latin, with which his surprising memory was richly stored; and I cannot think that he could resist the temptation of introducing them into his discourse from the pulpit, yet I heard no hint of this in the only sermon of his which was repeated to me by one of his congregation. The occasion of its delivery was this.

He was highly incensed at a long engagement being broken off between some young people in his parish, so next Sunday he preached on "Let love be without dissimulation;" and the sermon, which on this occasion was extempore, was reported by those who heard it to consist of little more than this—"You see, my dearly beloved brethren, what the Apostle says—Let love be without dissimulation. Now I'll tell y' what I think dissimulation is. When a young chap goes out a walking with a girl,—as nice a lass as ever you saw, with an uncommon fresh pair o' cheeks and pretty black eyes too, and not a word against her character, very respectably brought up,—when, I say, my dearly beloved brethren, a young chap goes out walking with such a young woman, after church of a summer evening, seen of every one, and offers her his arm, and they look friendly like at each other, and at times he buys her a present at the fair, a ribbon, or a bit of jewellery—I cannot say I have heard, and I don't say that I have seen,—when, I say, dearly beloved brethren, a young chap like this goes on for more than a year, and lets everybody fancy they are going to be married,—I don't mean to say that at times a young chap may see a nice lass and admire her, and talk to her a bit, and then go away and forget her—there's no dissimulation in that;—but when it goes on a long time, and he makes her to think he's very sweet upon her, and that he can't live without her, and he gives her ribbons and jewellery that I can't particularize, because I haven't seen them—when a young chap, dearly beloved brethren—" and so on and so on, becoming more and more involved. The parties preached about were in the church, and the young man was just under the pulpit, with the eyes of the whole congregation turned on him. The sermon had its effect—he reverted to his love, and without any dissimulation, we trust, married her.

The Christmas and the Easter decorations in this old fellow's church were very wonderful. There was a Christmas text, and that did service also for Easter. The decorating of the church was intrusted to the schoolmaster, a lame man, and his wife, and consisted in a holly or laurel crutch set up on one side of the chancel, and a "jaws of death" on the other. This appalling symbol was constructed like a set of teeth in a dentist's shop-window—the fangs were made of snipped or indented white drawing paper, and the gums of overlapping laurel leaves stitched down one on the other.

A very good story was told of this old parson, which is, I believe, quite true. He was invited to spend a couple of days with a great squire some miles off. He went, stayed his allotted time, and disappeared. Two days later the lady of the house, happening to go into the servants'-hall in the evening, found, to her amazement, her late guest—there. After he had finished his visit up-stairs, at the invitation of the butler he spent the same time below. "Like Persephone, madam," he said,—"half my time above, half in the nether world."

In the matter of personal neatness he left much to be desired. His walled garden was famous for its jargonelle pears. Lady X—, one day coming over, said to him, "Will you come back in my carriage with me, and dine at the Park? You can stay the night, and be driven home to-morrow."

"Thank you, my lady, delighted. I will bring with me some jargonelles. I'll go and fetch them."

Presently he returned with a little open basket and some fine pears in it. Lady X— looked at him, with a troubled expression in her sweet face. The rector was hardly in dining suit; moreover, there was apparent no equipment for the night.

"Dear Mr. M—, will you not really want something further? You will dine with us, and sleep the night."

A vacant expression stole over his countenance, as he retired into himself in thought. Presently a flash of intelligence returned, and he said with briskness, "Ah! to be sure; I'll go and fetch two or three more jargonelles."

A kind, good-hearted man the scholar-parson was, always ready to put his hand into his pocket at a tale of distress, but quite incapable of understanding that his parishioners might have spiritual as well as material requirements. I remember a case of a very similar man—a fellow of his college, and professor at Cambridge—to whom a young student ventured to open some difficulties and doubts that tortured him. "Difficulties! doubts!" echoed the old gentleman. "Take a couple of glasses of port. If that

58

don't dispel them, take two more, and continue the dose till you have found ease of mind."

But to return to our country parson, who had the jargonelles. His church was always well attended. Quite as large a congregation was to be found in it as in other parish churches, where all the modern appliances of music, popular preaching, parish visitations, clubs and bible-classes were in force. Perhaps the reason was that he was not too spiritually exacting. Many of our enthusiastic modern parsons attempt to screw up their people into a condition of spiritual exaltation which they are quite unable to maintain permanently, and then they become discouraged at the inevitable, invariable relapse.

We suppose that one main cause of dissent is the deadness and dulness of the Church service before the revival of late days; and we attribute this deadness and dulness to the indifference of these bêtes noirs, the clergy of last century. I doubt it.

At the time of the Commonwealth our churches had been gutted of everything ornamental and beautiful, and the services reduced to the most dreary performance of sermon and extempore prayer. At the Restoration, a very large number indeed of the Presbyterian ministers conformed, were ordained, and retained the benefices. Naturally they conducted the Common Prayer as nearly as they could on the lines of the service they were accustomed to. They had no tradition of what the Anglican liturgy was; they did not understand it, and they served it up cold or lukewarm, as unpalatable as possible. They did not like it themselves, and they did not want their congregations to become partial to it. The old clergy who were restored were obliged to content themselves with the merest essentials of Divine worship; their congregations had grown up without acquaintance with the liturgy—at all events for some nineteen years they had not heard it, and they did not want to shock their weak consciences by too sudden a transformation.

When Pepys went to church on November 4, 1660, he entered in his Diary, "Mr. Mills did begin to nibble at the Common Prayer, by saying Glory be to the Father, &c., after he had read the two psalms; but the people had been so little used to it, that they could not tell what to answer." The same afternoon he went to Westminster Abbey, "where the first time that ever I heard the organs in a cathedral."

Evelyn enters, on March 22, 1678, "now was our Communion-table placed altar-wise," that is to say, not till eighteen years after the Restoration! so slowly were alterations made in the churches to bring them back to their former conditions of decency and order.

Whatever has been done since has been done cautiously and with hesitation, lest offence should be given.

It was not practicable in our village churches to have the hearty congregational singing that now prevails, for only a very few could read, and only such could join in the psalmody.

I have in my possession a diary kept by a kinswoman in 1813. She makes in that year an entry, "Walked over this Sunday to South Mimms church to hear a barrel-organ that has just been there erected. It made very beautiful and appropriate music, and admirably sustained the voices of the quire, but I do not myself admire these innovations in the conduct of Divine worship." What would she have said to the innovations that have taken place since then, had she lived to see them! And they have been, for the most part, in a right direction; but we must be thankful, not only for them, but for the evidence they give that the clergy are somewhat emerging from that condition in which they were, as Crabbe describes them, when "Fear was their ruling passion"—

> "All things new
> Were deemed superfluous, useless, or untrue.
> Habit with him was all the test of truth;
> It must be right; I've done it from my youth.
> Questions he answer'd in as brief a way;—
> It must be wrong—it was of yesterday."

CHAPTER VI

THE HUNTING PARSON

WHY not? why should not the parson mount his cob and go after the hounds? A more fresh, invigorating pursuit is not to be found, not one in which he is brought more in contact with his fellow-men. There was a breezy goodness about many a hunting parson of the old times that was in itself a sermon, and was one on the topic that healthy amusement and Christianity go excellently well together. I had rather any day see a parson ride along with the pink, than sport the blue ribbon. The last of our genuine West Country hunting parsons was Jack Russell, whose life has already been written, but to whom I can bear testimony that he was a good specimen of the race. I was one day on top of a coach along with two farmers, one from the parish of Jack Russell, another from that of another hunting parson, whom we will call Jack Hannaford. They were discussing their relative parsons. Then he who was under Hannaford told a scurvy tale of him, whereat his companion said, "Tell'ee what, all the world knows what your pa'sson be; but as for old Jack Russell, up and down his backbone, he's as good a Christian, as worthy a pastor, and as true a gentleman as I ever seed."

In a parish on the Cornish side of the estuary of the Tamar, some little while ago, the newly appointed rector, turning over the register of baptisms in the vestry, was much astonished at seeing entries of the christening of boys only. "Why, Richard!" said he to the clerk, "however comes this about—are there only boys born in this place?"

"Please your Reverence, 'tain't that; but as they won't take the girls into the dockyard at Devonport, 'tain't no good baptizing 'em." The boys were christened only for the sake of the register requisite to present on admission into the Government dockyard. But if the boys were given baptism only, the girls devoted their efforts to show that they fell behind in masculine gifts in no sort, and the women of the village have approved themselves remarkable Amazons; they pull a boat, carry loads, speak gruff, wear moustache, very much as does a man.

Now, the unfortunate thing is, that the English clergy of the new epoch do seem to have been only ordained because they are feeble and effeminate youths. After ordination the curates are thrust into the society of pious and feeble women, and contract feeble and womanish ways. Just as in the Cornish parish only boys were baptized, so does it really seem as though only girlish youngsters pass under the bishop's hands, so that ordination becomes a pledge of effeminacy. Therefore, in my opinion, it would be a wholesome corrective if they could go after the hounds occasionally.

It is one thing to make of hunting a pursuit, and another to take it as a relaxation. The apostles were sportsmen, that is to say, they fished; and if it is lawful to go after fish, I take it there can be no harm in going after a hare or a fox; but then—only occasionally, and as a moral and constitutional bracer.

As said of the ordinary country parson, the good is forgotten and the evil is remembered, so is it with the hunting parson. The simple worthy rector who attended his sick, was good to the poor, preached a wholesome sermon, and was seen occasionally at the meet, is not remembered,—Jack Russell is the exception,—but the memory of the bad hunting parson never dies.

There is a characteristic song about the typical indifferent hunting parson that was much sung some fifty years ago. It ran thus—[7]

PARSON HOGG

Arranged by the Rev. H. Fleetwood Sheppard, M.A.

Mess Parson Hogg shall now maintain
The burden of my song, sir!
A single life perforce he led,
Of constitution strong, sir.
Sing tally ho! sing tally ho!
sing tally ho! why zounds, sir!
He mounts his mare to hunt the hare,
Sing Tally ho! the hounds, sir.

And every day he goes to mass
He first pulls on his boot, sir!
That, should the beagles chance to pass,
He may join in the pursuit, sir!
Sing, Tally ho! &c.

---

[7] From Songs of the West: Traditional Songs and Ballads of the West of England. Collected by S. Baring Gould and H. Fleetwood Sheppard. London: Methuen & Co. 1889.

That Parson little loveth prayer,
And pater night and morn, sir!
For bell and book hath little care,
But dearly loves the horn, sir!
Sing, Tally ho! &c.

St. Stephen's day that holy man
He went a pair to wed, sir!
When as the service was begun,
Puss by the churchyard sped, sir!
Sing, Tally ho! &c.

He shut his book. "Come on," he said,
"I'll pray and bless no more, sir!"
He drew the surplice o'er his head,
And started for the door, sir!
Sing, Tally ho! &c.

In pulpit Parson Hogg was strong,
He preached without a book, sir!
And to the point, but never long,
And this the text he took, sir!
O Tally ho! O Tally ho!
Dearly Beloved—zounds, sir!
I mount my mare to hunt the hare,
Singing, Tally ho! the hounds, sir!

One of the very worst types of the hunting parson was that man Chowne, whom Mr. Blackmore has immortalized in his delightful story of The Maid of Sker. Many of the tales told in that novel relative to Chowne—the name of course is fictitious—are quite true. As I happen to know a good many particulars of the life of this man, I will here give them.

He was rector of a wild lonely parish situated on high ground—ground so high that trees did not flourish about the rectory, nor did flowers thrive in his garden. Flowers in Chowne's garden! the idea is inconceivable. The people were wild and rough in those days, especially so in that storm-beaten, almost Alpine spot, accessible still only by abominable roads up hill and down dale, like riding over the waves of a stormy sea. They were not, therefore, particularly shocked at their parson's lack of sweetness and light. Probably, if they thought anything about this, they considered that sweetness and light were as ill adapted to

Blackamoor as lilies and roses. His force of character impressed them, and commanded and obtained respect. To shock moral feelings, moral feelings must first exist. The parson was not disliked, he was feared. A curious man he was in appearance, with eyes hard, boring, dark, that made a man on whom they were fixed shiver to his toes. The parishioners believed he had the evil eye, and "overlooked" or "ill-wished" those whom he desired to injure, or any one who had given him offence. There is no breaking such a spell save by drawing the blood of the "over-looker," and no one was hardy enough to attempt this of Chowne. When a woman is thought to have cast a spell through her malignant eye, the person that suffers scratches the inflicter of evil.

The story told in The Maid of Sker, of Chowne breaking up the road to prevent the bishop visiting him, is true. Dr. Phillpotts was then bishop, and he was eminently dissatisfied with what he heard of the ecclesiastical and moral condition of Blackamoor and its parson. He therefore drove there to make a personal visitation. Chowne, forewarned, employed men to dig up the road for a space of about twenty feet, and the hole they made was filled in with bog-water, then the whole lightly covered over with turf and strewn with dust. The Bishop's carriage and horses floundered in and was upset. Henry of Exeter was, however, not the man to be daunted by such an accident—that it was not an accident, but a deliberate attempt to stay his course, he saw at once by the condition of the road. He went on to Blackamoor, and reached the parsonage. There he found Chowne in his dining-room, sullen, with his wicked black eyes watching him. His head was for the most part bald, but he had one long wisp of dark hair that he twisted about his bald pate. Chowne put a bottle of brandy on the table, and a couple of tumblers, and bade the Bishop help himself.

"No, thank you, Mr. Chowne," said the Bishop briefly.

"Ah! my lord, you may do without it, maybe, at Exeter, but up at this height we must drink or perish of dulness."

Then he helped himself to a stiff glass, and relapsed into silence. Presently the Bishop said—

"You keep hounds, I hear."

"No, my lord, the hounds keep me."

"I do not understand."

"Well, then, you must be mighty stupid. They stock my larder with hares. You don't suppose I should have hares on my table unless they were caught for me. There's no butcher for miles and miles, and I can't get a joint but once in a fortnight maybe; what should I do without rabbits and hares? Forced to eat 'em, and they must be caught to be eaten."

"Mr. Chowne," said Henry of Exeter, "I've been told that you have men in here with you drinking and fighting."

"It's a lie. I admit that they drink,—every man drinks since he was a baby,—but fight in my dining-room! No, my lord! Directly they begin to fight I take 'em by the scruff of the neck, and turn them out into the churchyard, and let 'em fight out their difference among the tombs."

"I am sorry to say, Mr. Chowne, that I have heard some very queer and unsatisfactory tales concerning you."

"I dare say you have, my lord;" he fixed his strong eyes on the Bishop. "So have I of your lordship, very unpleasant and nasty tales, when I've been to Torrington or Bideford fairs. But when I do, I say it's a parcel of —— lies. And when next you hear any of these tales about me, then you say, 'I know Tom Chowne very well—drunk out of his bottle of brandy—I swear that all these tales about him is also a parcel of lies."

The story is told in The Maid of Sker of his having driven a horse mad by putting a hemp-grain into its eye. That story is thought to be true. The horse was one he coveted, but it was bought at a higher figure than he cared to give for it by Sir Walter C——. Chowne shortly after was at a fair or market where Sir Walter was, who had ridden in on this very horse. He slipped out of the inn and into the stable, just before the Baronet left, and thus treated the unfortunate animal, which went almost mad with the pain, and threw his rider.

He had certain men in the parish, not exactly in his pay, but so completely under his control, that they executed his suggestions without demur, whatever they might be, and never for a moment gave thought that they themselves were free agents. As Henry II. did not order the murder of Becket, but threw out a hint that it would be an acceptable thing to him to be rid of the proud prelate, so was it with Chowne. He never ordered the commission of a crime, but he suggested the commission. For instance, if a farmer had offended him, he would say to one of these men subject to his influence, "As I've been standing in the church porch, Harry, I thought what a terrible thing it would be if the rick of Farmer Greenaway which I can see over against me were to burn. 'Twould come home to him pretty sharp, I reckon." Next night the rick would be on fire. Or he would say to his groom, "Tom, there's Farmer Moyle going to sup with me at the parsonage to-night. Shocking thing were his linchpin to be gone, and as he was going down Blackamoor hill, the wheel were to come off."

That night he would entertain Moyle with unwonted

cordiality, pass the bottle freely, whilst an ominous spark burnt in his pebbly eye. As the farmer that night drove away, his wheel would come off, and he be thrown, and be found by the next passer along the road with dislocated thigh or broken arm and collar-bone.

As already said, he kept a pack of harriers, but in such a wretched, rattletrap set of kennels that they occasionally broke loose. This occurred once on Sunday, and just as Chowne was going to the pulpit, the pack went by. He halted with his hand on the banister, turned to the clerk, and said, "That's Towler giving voice. Run—he's got the lead, and will tear the hare to bits."

Thereupon forth went the clerk, and succeeded in securing the hare from the hounds hunting on their own head. He brought the hare into church, and threw it under his seat till the sermon was done, the blessing given, and the congregation dismissed.

Chowne had a housekeeper named Sally. One day Chowne came down very smartly dressed.

"Where be you a-going to to-day?" asked Sally.

"That's no concern of yours," answered the rector; "but I don't mind telling you either—I'm going to be married."

"Why! for sure, you're not going to be such a fool as that!" exclaimed the housekeeper.

"I don't know but what it may be a folly," growled Chowne; "but, Sally, it's a folly you are bent on committing too."

To this Sally, who for some time had been keeping company with one Joe, made no reply.

"Now look'ye here," said Chowne. "I don't want you to marry, Sally. It's no reason because I make a fool o' myself, that you should go and do likewise."

"But why not, master?"

"Because I want'y to stay here and see that my wife don't maltreat me," answered Chowne. "And I'll tell'y what, Sally—if you'll give up Joe, I'll give thee the fat pig. Which will'y now prefer, Joe or the porker?"

Sally considered for a moment, and then said, "Lauk! sir, I'd rayther have the pig."

And now must be told how it was that Chowne was brought to the marriage state.

There was in the neighbourhood a yeoman family named Heathman, and there was a handsome daughter belonged to the house. Chowne had paid her some of his insolent attentions, that meant, if they meant anything, some contemptuous admiration. Her brothers were angry. It was reported that Chowne had spoken of their sister, moreover, in a manner they would not brook; so they invited him to their house, made him drunk, and when drunk sign a paper promising to marry Jane Heathman before three months were up, or to forfeit £10,000. They took care to have this document well attested, and next morning presented it to Chowne, who had forgotten all about it. He was much put out, blustered, cajoled, tried to laugh it off—all to no purpose. The brothers insisted on his either taking Jane to wife, or paying the stipulated sum. He asked for delay, and rode off to consult his friend Hannaford.

"Bless 'y," said Hannaford, "ten thousand pounds is a terrible big sum to pay. Take the creature."

Thus it came about that Chowne yielded to the less disagreeable alternative. Poor Jane Heathman! she little thought of what was in store for her. Her brothers had shown her a cruel kindness in forcing her into the arms of a reluctant suitor.

To return to the wedding day, after the offer made to and accepted by Sally.

About one o'clock Chowne returned alone, seated himself composedly in his dining-room, and ordered dinner.

"But where be the wife?" asked Sally. "Haven't 'ee been married then?"

"Aye, married I have been, though."

"But where be Mistress Chowne?"

"She's at the public-house good three miles from here, Sally. She said to me as we were coming along, 'That is a point on which I differ from you.' Some point on which we were speaking. So I stopped, and looked her in the face, and I said to her, 'Mrs. Chowne, I never allow any one outside my house to differ from me, and not everlastingly repent it afterwards. And I won't allow any one inside my house to differ from me. So you can remain at this tavern and turn the matter over in your mind. If you intend to have no will of your own, and no opinion other than mine, then you can walk on at your leisure to Blackamoor. If not, you can turn back and go home to where you came from. Nobody expects you at Blackamoor, and nobody wants you there. So you are heartily welcome to keep away. So—serve the dinner, Sally, for one."

An hour and a half later the bride arrived on foot, forlorn and humbled, and met with an ungracious reception from Sally.

Sally had the pig that had been promised her killed, cut up, and sold. After a while Chowne suspected that she was still keeping company with Joe. He was very angry, for he felt that he had been done out of the pig on false pretences; so he went off with his wife to stay with Parson Hannaford, and gave out he would not return for a week. On the second evening, however, he suddenly returned, and came bounding in at the door; and sure enough Joe was there, come courting, and to eat his supper with Sally. The housekeeper, hearing the tread of her master, bade Joe fly and get out of his reach. But the back-door was fastened, and Joe, in his alarm, jumped into the copper. Sally put the lid on, and dashed into the passage to meet her master.

"Where's Joe? I'm sure he's here. You've cut too much of my ham to fry for yourself alone. You've drawn too much ale. I'm sure Joe is here!" shouted Chowne, looking about him.

"Deary life, sir!" exclaimed the housekeeper, "I protest! I don't know where he can be. Why, master, you know I gave him up for the sake of the pig."

Chowne's eye wandered about the kitchen, and noticed—what was unusual—the lid on the copper in the adjoining back-kitchen, that served also as laundry.

"Sally," said he, "put some water into the copper to boil. I'm going to dip the pups. They've got the mange."

"Ain't there enough in the kettle, master?"

"No, there is not. Put water into the copper."

Accordingly Sally was forced to fill a can at the pump, and pour water into the copper over her lover, removing for the purpose only a corner of the cover.

"There, master. Do'y let me serve you up some supper, and I'll get the water heated after."

"No," said Chowne, "I'll stand here till it boils. Shove in some browse" (light firewood).

Reluctantly the browse was put in under the cauldron, and was lighted. It flared up.

"Now some hard wood, Sally," said the parson.

Still more reluctantly were sawn logs inserted. A moment after up went the copper lid, and out scrambled Joe, hot and dripping.

"Ah! I reckoned you was there," shouted Chowne, and went at him with his horse-whip, and lashed the fellow about the kitchen, down the passage, into the hall, and out at the front door, where he dismissed him with a kick.

I tell the tale as it was told to me, but I suspect the conclusion of this story. It reminds me of a familiar folk-tale. But then—is it not the prerogative of such tales to attach themselves to the last human notoriety?

That this same crop, or hunting-whip, was applied to Mrs. Chowne's shoulders and back was commonly reported in Blackamoor, and indeed is so reported even unto this day.

The following story is on the authority of Jack Russell, Vicar of Swimbridge. He had called one day at Blackamoor parsonage, and found Chowne sitting over his fire smoking, and Mrs. Chowne sitting in one corner of the room, against the wall. Her husband had turned his back on her. Russell was uneasy, and asked if Mrs. Chowne were unwell. Chowne turned his head over his shoulder and asked, "Mrs. Chowne, be you satisfied or be you not? You know the terms of agreement come to between us. If you are not satisfied, you can go home to your friends, and I won't hinder you from going. I don't care a hang myself whether you stay or whether you go."

"I am content," said the lady faintly.

"Very well," said Chowne. "Then we'll have a drop of cider, Jack. Go and fetch us a jug and tumblers, madam."

In The Maid of Sker Chowne is represented as torn to pieces by his hounds. The real Chowne did not meet this fate. His death was, however, tragic in another aspect. He had left his rectory, and lived in a more sheltered spot in a house of his own. Before the windows grew a particularly handsome box-tree. Now Chowne had done some dastardly mean and cruel act to a young farmer near, tricking him out of a large sum of money in a way peculiarly base.

One night the box-tree was taken up and carried away, no one knew whither, though every one suspected by whom. Chowne raged over this insult; and as he was unable to bring the act home to the culprit, his rage was impotent. But the uprooting of the box-tree was apparently the death of him. He felt that the dread he had inspired was gone, his control over the neighbourhood was lost, the spell of his personality was broken. This thought, even more than mortified rage at being unable to discover and punish the man who had pulled up his box-tree, broke him down, and he rapidly sank, intellectually and physically, into a ruin, and died.

Chowne had a friend, a man, if possible, worse than himself, him whom we will call Jack Hannaford, who was Vicar of Wellclose. It was said that Hannaford was brutal, but Chowne fiendish.

Hannaford was an immensely powerful man. He said one day to his groom, "Come on, Bill, we'll go over to Bidlake and take a rise out of Welford"—afterwards Lord Lundy. So they blackened their faces, disguised themselves in cast-off clothes, and went to the lodge at Bidlake. They were denied admittance, but forced their way in and walked up the drive. The lodge-keeper ran after them and attacked the groom, who at once buckled-to for a fight. Then a couple of keepers burst out from the shrubbery.

"Leave them alone," said Hannaford. "It's a pretty sight. Don't interfere to spoil sport."

However, one of the keepers went at the groom, to the relief of the lodge-keeper.

"Oh, you will, will you," said Hannaford. He caught him with his huge hand and cast him on the gravel. The other keeper fared no better. The groom had in the meantime demolished his man; so he and his master sauntered along the drive without further molestation till they reached the house. Hannaford went to the door to ring, when the Hon. Mr. Welford appeared, and angrily inquired what was their business.

"Work, your honour," answered Hannaford, pulling a forelock.

"Work is it you want? But did not my keepers stop your coming up this way?"

"They tried it, but they couldn't do it," answered Hannaford. "There they be—skulking along."

"They could not stop you?"

"We flung three of them in the road," answered Hannaford. "And now I reckon your honour will give us something to drink your health."

Mr. Welford gave them a crown and dismissed them—also, it is said, the keepers. If so, that was hardly fair, for Hannaford was the strongest man in England. He was beaten but once, and that was in Exeter, when drunk. He had gone over to the city for a spree, and had put up at a low public-house. There he met with a Welshman, and had a fight with him, and was horribly mauled about the head and body. Next day, when sober, Hannaford followed the man by train to Bristol, and thence tracked him to some little out-of-the-way place in Wales. He proceeded to his door, knocked, called the man out, and fought him there and then—and this time utterly thrashed him. When the fellow was so knocked about that he could not speak and hold up, "There," said the Devonshire parson, "now take care how you lay a finger on Jack Hannaford again when he is drunk. If you wish for a return bout, call at your will at Wellclose Parsonage, and you'll find him ready."

Some years ago a famous prize-fighter went about England on exhibition. He came to Taunton, but was there taken ill, and unable to show himself. The manager at once wrote or telegraphed to Jack Hannaford, and he went up with alacrity to supply his place. He was stripped, showed his muscles, and his mode of hitting, as the advertised pugilist. The Taunton people would have been none the wiser, but, as it happened, Lord Lundy was in the tent. Hannaford caught his eye, and saw that he was recognized; so he went over to his lordship and whispered, "Mum, my lord. The second best man in

England was laid on the shelf, so they had to telegraph for the best man to take his place."

Hannaford would never give any pocket-money to his sons till they were strong enough to knock him down. Then each received a five-pound note, which he was considered at length to have deserved by having made proof of his manhood.

It is a fact that on market days, when Hannaford was seen on the platform with his ticket for the market town, the farmers would bribe the guard to put him into a carriage by himself and lock him in, so afraid were they of being in the same compartment with the parson, who would challenge and fight a man in a railway carriage as readily as anywhere else.

Though a hunting parson, of altogether different character was Jack Russell. He was a sporting man to the end of his fingers and toes, but a most worthy, kind-hearted, God-fearing, righteous man.

One story of Jack Russell that is not, I believe, told in his Life, is worth repeating. When he was over eighty, he started keeping a pack of harriers. The then Bishop of Exeter sent for him.

"Mr. Russell, I hear you have got a pack of hounds. Is it true?"

"It is. I won't deny it, my lord."

"Well, Mr. Russell, it seems to me rather unsuitable for a clergyman to keep a pack. I do not ask you to give up hunting, for I know it would not be possible for you to exist without that. But will you, to oblige me, give up the pack?"

"Do'y ask it as a personal favour, my lord?"

"Yes, Mr. Russell, as a personal favour."

"Very well, then, my lord, I will."

"Thank you, thank you." The Bishop, moved by his readiness, held out his hand. "Give me your hand, Mr. Russell; you are—you really are—a good fellow."

Jack Russell gave his great fist to the Bishop, who pressed it warmly. As they thus stood hand in hand, Jack said,

"I won't deceive you—not for the world, my lord. I'll give up the pack, sure enough—but Mrs. Russell will keep it instead of me."

The Bishop dropped his hand.

That men like Chowne and Hannaford were unpopular in their parishes I have never heard. I do not believe they were troubled with any aggrieved parishioners. The unpopular man in his parish is he who tries to raise the moral and spiritual tone of his people. They do not like to be made to think that all is not well with them, and it affords them satisfaction to think that they are not worse, if no better, than their pastor.

71

I know a parish in quite another part of England where the attendance at church was very thin, till the incumbent was one day accidentally, I believe, overtaken with drink, and was had up before the magistrates. After that his church filled, he became a popular man—he had come down to the level of his people.

But, as already said, it is of the bad parsons, as of the bad squires, that stories are told, and told from generation to generation; whereas those of spotless life—the vast bulk of them are such—drop year by year out of existence, and at the same time out of memory.

In the parish in which I live there was a rector, about seventy years ago, who in his old age went to the neighbouring town, nine miles off, to live, and when asked by the Bishop why he was non-resident, said that there was no barber nearer who could curl his wig.

That man held the living for a long term of years; he may have done good,—that he did evil I do not think, because the only thing remembered against him is, that he did not live in a place where his wig could not be curled. But is it not sad!—a long life's labour spent among the poor, preaching God's word, ministering to the sick and afflicted and broken-hearted, and all passing away without leaving the smallest trace, indeed the only reminiscence of the man being, that he hurt the amour propre of the parish by telling the Bishop there was no one in it competent to curl his wig.

CHAPTER VII

COUNTRY DANCES

CLISTHENES, tyrant of Sicyon, says Herodotus, had a beautiful daughter whom he resolved to marry to the most accomplished of the Greeks. Accordingly all the eligible young men of Greece resorted to the court of Sicyon to offer for the hand of the lovely Agarista. Among these, the most distinguished was Hippoclides, and the king decided to take him as his son-in-law.

Clisthenes had already invited the guests to the nuptial feast, and had slaughtered one hundred oxen to the gods to obtain a blessing on the union, when Hippoclides offered to exhibit the crown and climax of his many accomplishments.

He ordered a flute-player to play a dance tune, and when the musician obeyed, he (Hippoclides) began to dance before the king and court and guests, and danced to his own supreme satisfaction.

After the first bout, and he had rested awhile and recovered breath, he ordered a table to be introduced, and he danced figures on it, and finally set his head on the table and gesticulated with his legs.

When the applause had ceased, Clisthenes said—as the young man had reverted to his feet and stood expectantly before him— "You have danced very well, but I don't want a dancing son-in-law."

How greatly we should like to know what Herodotus does not tell us, whether the tyrant of Sicyon was of a sour and puritanical mind, objecting to dancing on principle, or whether he objected to the peculiar kind of dance performed by Hippoclides, notably that with his head on the table and his legs kicking in the air.

I do not think that such a thing existed at that period as puritanical objection to dancing, but I imagine that it was the sort of dance which offended Clisthenes. Lucian in one of his Dialogues introduces a philosopher who reproaches a friend for being addicted to dancing, whereupon the other replies that dancing was of Divine invention, for the goddess Rhæa first composed set dances about the infant Jupiter to hide him from the eyes of his father Saturn, who wanted to eat him. Moreover, Homer speaks with high respect of dancing, and declares that the grace and nimbleness of Merion in the dance distinguished him above the rest of the heroes in the contending hosts of Greeks and Trojans. He adds that in Greece statues were erected to the honour of the best dancers, so highly was the art held in repute, and that Hesiod places on one footing valour and dancing, when he says that "The gods have bestowed fortitude on some men, and on others a disposition for dancing!" Lastly, he puts the philosopher in mind that Socrates not only admired the saltatory exercise in others, but learned it himself when he was an old man.

On hearing this defence of dancing, the morose philosopher in Lucian's Dialogue professes himself a convert, and requests his friend to take him to the next subscription ball.

Steele, in the Spectator, declared that "no one ever was a good dancer that had not a good understanding," and that it is an art whereby mechanically, so to speak, "a sense of good-breeding and virtue are insensibly implanted in minds not capable of receiving it so well in any other rules."

I cannot help thinking that the dancing commended by the Spectator, learned in old age by Socrates, and that in which the Greeks won the honour of statues, was something far removed from that which incurred the displeasure of Clisthenes, and lost Hippoclides the hand of his beautiful mistress.

Here is a letter in the Spectator, given in Steele's article. It purports to be from a father, Philipater: "I am a widower, with one daughter; she was by nature much inclined to be a romp, and I had no way of educating her, but commanding a young woman, whom I entertained to take care of her, to be very watchful in her care and attendance about her. I am a man of business and obliged to be much abroad. The neighbours have told me, that in my absence our maid has let in the spruce servants in the neighbourhood to junketings, while my girl play'd and romped even in the street. To tell you the plain truth, I catched her once, at eleven years old, at chuck-farthing, among the boys. This put me upon new thoughts about my child, and I determined to place her at a boarding-school. I took little notice of my girl from time to time, but saw her now and then in good health, out of harm's way, and was satisfied. But by much importunity, I was lately prevailed with to go to one of their balls. I cannot express to you the anxiety my silly heart was in, when I saw my romp, now fifteen, taken out. I could not have suffered more, had my whole fortune been at stake. My girl came on with the most becoming modesty I had ever seen, and casting a respectful eye, as if she feared me more than all the audiency, I gave a nod, which, I think, gave her all the spirit she assumed upon it, but she rose properly to that dignity of aspect. My romp, now the most graceful person of her sex, assumed a majesty which commanded the highest respect. You, Mr. Spectator, will, better than I can tell you, imagine all the different beauties and changes of aspect in an accomplished young woman, setting forth all her beauties with a design to please no one so much as her father. My girl's lover can never know half the satisfaction that I did in her that day. I could not possibly have imagined that so great improvement could have been wrought by an art that I always held in itself ridiculous and contemptible. There is, I am convinced, no method like this, to give young women a sense of their own value and dignity; and I am sure there can be none so expeditious to communicate that value to others. For my part, my child has danced herself into my esteem, and I have as great an honour of her as ever I had for her mother, from whom she derived those latent good qualities which appeared in her countenance when she was dancing; for my girl showed in one quarter of an hour the innate principles of a modest virgin, a tender wife, and generous friend, a kind mother, and an indulgent mistress."

It is a curious fact that the beautiful and graceful dance, the dance as a fine art, is extinct among us. It has been expelled by the intrusive waltz. And if in the waltz any of that charm of modesty, grace of action, and dignity of posture can be found, which delighted our forefathers and made them esteem dancing, then let it be shown. It was not waltzing which made Merion to be esteemed among the heroes of the Trojan war; it was not waltzing certainly that Socrates acquired in his old age; and it most assuredly was not whilst she was waltzing that the correspondent of the Spectator admired in his daughter the modest virgin. It is possible that it was a sort of topsy-turvy waltz Hippoclides performed, and which lost him the daughter of Clisthenes.

The dance is not properly the spinning around of two persons of opposite sex hugging each other, and imitating the motion of a teetotum. The dance is an assemblage of graceful movements and figures performed by a set number of persons. There is singular beauty in the dance proper. The eye is pleased by a display of graceful and changing outline, by bringing into play the muscles of well-moulded limbs. But where many performers take part the enchantment is increased, just as part-singing is more lovely than solo-singing; for to the satisfaction derived from the graceful attitude of one performer is added that of beautiful grouping. A single well-proportioned figure is a goodly sight; several well-proportioned figures in shifting groups, now in clusters, now swinging loose in wreaths, now falling into line or circles; whilst an individual, or a pair, focus the interest, is very beautiful. It is the change in a concert from chorus to solo; and when, whilst the single dance, projected into prominence, attracts the delighted eye, the rest of the dancers keep rhythmic motion, subdued, in simple change, the effect is exquisite. It is the accompaniment on a living instrument to a solo.

A correspondent of the Times recently gave us an account of the Japanese ballet, which illustrates what I insist on. He tells us that the Maikos or Japanese ballet-dancers are girls of from sixteen to eighteen years of age; they wear long fine silk dresses, natural flowers in their hair, and hold fans in their hands. Their dance is perfectly decorous, exquisitely graceful, and of marvellous artistic beauty. It partakes of the nature of the minuet and the gavotte; it makes no violent demands on lungs and muscles; its object is to give pleasure to the spectators through the exhibition of harmony of lines, elegance of posture, beauty of dress, grace with which the folds of the long drapery fall, the play of light, and change of arrangement of colour. It is a dance full of noble and stately beauty, and has nothing in common with our European ballet, with its extravagance and indelicacy, and—it must be added—inelegance. It is a play without words, and a feast of pure delight to the artistic eye.

Æsthetically, the dance is, or may be, one of the most beautiful creations of man, an art, and an art of no mean order. In it each man and woman has to sustain a part, is one of many, a member of a company, enchained to it by laws which all must obey. And yet each has in his part a certain scope for individual expansion, for the exercise of liberty. It is a figure of the world of men, in which each has a part to perform in relation to all the rest. If the performer uses his freedom to excess, the dancers in the social ball are thrown into disorder, and the beauty and unity of the performance is lost.

Now all this beauty is taken from us. The waltz has invaded our ball-rooms, and drives all other dances out of it. Next to the polka, the waltz is the rudest and most elementary of step and figure-dances; it has extirpated before it the lovely and intricate dances, highly artistic, and of elaborate organization, which were performed a century ago. How is it now in a ball? Even the quadrille and lancers, the sole remnants of an art beautiful to lookers-on, are sat out, or, after having been entered on the list, are omitted, and a waltz substituted for it. "Valse, valse, toujours valse!" A book on dances, published in 1821, speaks of the introduction of the waltz as a new thing, and of the rarity of finding persons at a ball who could dance it.

"The company at balls having no partners who are acquainted

with waltzing or quadrilles, generally become spectators of each other in a promenade round the rooms, so that the waltz or quadrille ball ends in country dances, sometimes not one of these dances being performed during the evening." That was a little over sixty years ago. Waltz and quadrille came in hand-in-hand, and displaced the old artistic and picturesque country dances, and then waltz prevailed, and kicked quadrille out at the door. The country dance is the old English dance—the dance of our forefathers—the dance which worked such wonders in the heart of the old father in Steele's paper in the Spectator.

The English have always been a dancing people, only during the Commonwealth did they kick their heels, dancing being unallowed; and at the beginning of this century dancing was discountenanced among the upper classes by the Evangelicals, and among villagers almost completely put down, or driven into low public-houses, by the Dissenters. In 1598 Hentzner describes the English as "excelling in dancing, and in the art of music;" and says that whilst a man might hope to become Lord Chancellor through dancing, without being bred to the law, like Sir Christopher Hatton, it was certainly worth while to endeavour to excel. According to Barnaby Rich, in 1581 the dances in vogue were measures—a grave and stately performance, like the minuet, galliards, jigs, braules, rounds, and hornpipes. In 1602 the Earl of Worcester writes to the Earl of Shrewsbury, "We are frolic here in Court, much dancing in the privy chamber of country dances before the Queen's Majesty, who is exceedingly pleased therewith." In the reign of James I., Waldon, sneering at Buckingham's kindred, observes that it is easier to put fine clothes on the back than to learn the French dances, and therefore that "none but country dances" must be used at Court. At Christmas, 1622-3, the Prince Charles "did lead the measures with the French ambassador's wife. The measures—braules, corrantoes, and galliards—being ended, the masquers with the ladies did dance two country dances."

In Pepys' Diary we read how he went to see the King dance in Whitehall. "By and by comes the King and Queen, the Duke (of York) and the Duchess, and all the great ones; and after seating themselves, the King takes out the Duchess of York; and the Duke, the Duchess of Buckingham; the Duke of Monmouth, my Lady Castlemaine; and so other lords other ladies; and they danced the Brantle. After that the King led a lady a single coranto; and then the rest of the lords, one after another, other ladies; very noble it was, and great pleasure to see. Then to country dances, the King leading the first, which he called for, which was, says he, 'Cuckolds all awry,' the old dance of England. Of the ladies that danced, the Duke of Monmouth's mistress, and my Lady Castlemaine, and a daughter of Sir Harry de Vicke's, were the best. The manner was, when the King dances, all the ladies in the room, and the Queen herself, stand up; and indeed, he dances rarely, and much better than the Duke of York. Having staid here as long as I thought fit, to my infinite content, it being the greatest pleasure I could wish now to see at Court, I went home, leaving them dancing."

All old ballads are set to dance tunes, and derive their name from ballet. Where no instruments were to be had, the dancers sang the ballad, and so gave the time to their feet. The fact of ballad tunes being dance tunes has been the occasion of their preservation; for in The Compleate Dancing Master, a collection of dance tunes, the first edition of which was published in 1650, and which went through eighteen editions to 1728, a great number have been preserved as dance tunes, with the titles of the ballads sung to them. In the old country dances the number of performers was unlimited, but could not consist of less than six.

What is the origin of our title for certain dances—"Country Dances"? I venture to think it has nothing to do with the country, though I have Chappell's weighty opinion against me. The designation was properly given to all those counter-dances, contredances, which were performed by the gentlemen standing on one side, and the ladies on the other, in lines, in contra-distinction to all round and square dances. As a general rule, foreign dances are circular or square. In Brittany is La Boulangère, and among the Basques, La Tapageuse, which are set in lines; but with a few exceptions, most continental dances were differentiated from the general type of English dances by being square or round. There were, no doubt, among our peasantry dances in a ring about the May-pole, but this was exceptional. A writer at the beginning of this century says,—"An English country dance differs from any other known dance in form and construction, except Ecossaise and quadrille country dances, as most others composed of a number of persons are either round, octagon, circular, or angular. The pastoral dances on the stage approximate the nearest to English country dances, being formed longways."

The song and the dance were closely associated; indeed, as already said, the word ballet is derived from "ballad," or vice-versâ; and all our old dance tunes had appropriate words set to them.

Dargason, a country dance older than the Reformation, found its way into Wales, where it was set to Welsh words; the English ballad to which it was usually sung was—

"It was a maid of my country,
As she came by a hawthorn tree,
As full of flowers as might be seen,
She marvelled to see the tree so green.
At last she asked of this tree
How came this freshness unto thee?
And every branch so fair and clean?
I marvel that you grow so green."

Doubtless half the charm of a country dance consisted in the dancers singing the words of the familiar ballad as they went through the movements of the dance, the burden often occurring at a general joining of hands and united movement.

An English country dance was composed of the putting together of several figures, and it allowed of almost infinite variation, according to the number and arrangement of the figures introduced. Sir Roger de Coverley, which is not quite driven out, consists of seven figures. Some figures are quite elementary, as turning the partner, setting, leading down the middle. Others are more elaborate, as Turn Corners, and Swing Corners; some are called Short Figures, as requiring in their performance a whole strain of short measure, or half a strain of long measure. Long Figures, on the other hand, occupy a strain of eight bars in long measure—a strain being that part of an air which is terminated by a double bar, and usually consists in country dances of four, eight, or sixteen single bars. Country dance tunes usually consist of two strains, though they sometimes extend to three, four, or five, and of eight bars each.

The names and character of the old country dances are quite forgotten.

The following is a list of some of the dances given in The Complete Country Dancing Master, published near the beginning of last century—

Whitehall.
Ackroyd's Pad.
The Whirligig.Amarillis.
Buttered Pease.
Bravo and Florimel.
Pope Joan.
Have at thy coat, old woman.
The Battle of the Boyne.
The Gossip's Frolic.

79

The Intrigue.
Prince and Princess.
A Health to Betty.
Bobbing Joan.
Sweet Kate.
Granny's Delight.
Essex Buildings.
Lord Byron's Maggot.
Ballamera.
The Dumps.
Rub her down with straw.
Moll Peatley.
Cheerily and Merrily.

In Waylet's Collection of Country Dances, published in 1749, we have these—

The Lass of Livingstone.
Highland Laddie.
Down the Burn, Davy.
Eltham Assembly.
Cephalus and Procris.
Joy go with her.
Duke of Monmouth's Jig.
Bonny Lass.
The Grasshopper.
The Pallet.
Jack Lattin.
Fiarnelle's Maggot.
Buttered Pease.
The Star.

Some of these dances were simplicity itself, consisting of only a very few elementary figures. This is the description of Sweet Kate.

"Lead up all a double and back. That again. Set your right foot to your woman's, then your left, clasp your woman on her right hand, then on the left, wind your hands and hold up your finger, wind your hands again and hold up another finger of the other hand, then single; and all this again."

Bobbing Joan is no more than this. First couple dance between the second, who then take their places, dance down, hands and all round, first two men snap fingers and change places, first women do the same, these two changes to the last, and the rest follow.

The tune of The Triumph is still found in collections of dance music, but it is only here and there in country places that it can be performed. I saw some old villagers of sixty and seventy years of age dance it last Christmas, but no young people knew anything about it. It is a slight, easy, but graceful dance—graceful when not danced by old gaffers and grannies.

Our English country dances were carried abroad, and became popular there. "The Italians," writes Horace Walpole from Florence in 1740, "are fond to a degree of our country dances: Cold and raw they only know by the tune; Blouzy-bella is almost Italian, and Buttered Peas is Pizzelli al buro." Indeed, as early as 1669, when the Grand Duke of Tuscany visited England, he was highly taken with the English dances, and probably on his return to Florence introduced them there. Count Lorenzo Magalotti, who attended him on his visit, says that he and the duke attended dancing-schools, "frequented by unmarried and married ladies, who are instructed by the master, and practise with much gracefulness and agility various dances after the English fashion. Dancing is a very common and favourite amusement of the ladies in this country; every evening there are entertainments at different places in the city, at which many ladies and citizens' wives are present, they going to them alone, as they do to the rooms of the dancing-masters, at which there are frequently upwards of forty or fifty ladies. His Highness had an opportunity of seeing several dances in the English style, exceedingly well regulated, and executed in the smartest and genteelest manner by very young ladies, whose beauty and gracefulness were shown off to perfection in this exercise." And again, "he went out to Highgate to see a children's ball, which, being conducted according to the English custom, afforded great pleasure to his Highness, both from the numbers, the manner, and the gracefulness of the dancers."

When our English country dances were carried abroad,—notably to Germany and France,—the tunes to which they were danced were carried with them, were there appropriated, and as these dances died out in their native home, and with them their proper melodies, the tunes have in several instances come back to us from the continent, as German or French airs.

Very probably one reason of the disapproval which country dancing has encountered arises from the fact that it allows no opportunities of conversation, and consequently of flirtation, as the partners stand opposite each other, and in the figures take part with other performers quite as much as with their own proper vis-à-vis. But then is a dance arranged simply to enable a young pair to clasp each other and whisper into each others ears? Are art, beauty, pleasure to the spectators to be left out of count altogether? The wall-fruit are deserving of commiseration, for they now see nothing that can gratify the eye in a ball-room; the waltz has been like the Norwegian rat—it has driven the native out altogether, and the native dance and the native rat were the more beautiful of the two.

It is not often we get a graceful dance on the stage either. Country dancing is banished thence also; distorted antics that are without grace, and of scanty decency, have supplanted it.

It seems incredible that what was regarded as a necessary acquisition of every lady and gentleman sixty or seventy years ago should have gone, and gone utterly—so utterly that probably dancing-masters of the present day would not know how to teach the old country dances. In The Complete System of Country Dancing, by Thomas Wilson, published about 1821 (there is no date on the title-page), the author insists on this being the national dance of the English, of its being in constant practice, of its being a general favourite "in every city and town throughout the United Kingdom;" as constituting "the principal amusement with the greater part of the inhabitants of this country." Not only so, but the English country dance was carried to all the foreign European Courts, where it "was very popular, and became the most favourite species of dancing;" and yet it is gone—gone utterly.

The minuet was, no doubt, a tedious and over-formal dance; it was only tolerable when those engaged wore hoops and powder and knee-breeches; but the English country dance is not stiff at all, and only so far formal as all complications of figures must be formal. It is at the same time infinitely elastic, for it allows of expansion or contraction by the addition or subtraction of figures. There are about a hundred figures in all, and these can be changed in place like the pieces of glass in a kaleidoscope.

Why, in this age of revivals, when we fill our rooms with Chippendale furniture and rococo mirrors and inlaid Florentine cabinets, and use the subdued colours of our grandmothers, when our books are printed in old type with head and tail pieces of two centuries ago, when the edges are left in the rough—why should we allow the waltz, the foreign waltz, to monopolize our ball-rooms to the exclusion of all beautiful figure-dancing, and let an old English art disappear completely without an attempt to recover it? It will be in these delightful, graceful, old national dances that our girls will, like the daughter of Philipater in the Spectator, dance themselves into our esteem, as it is pretty sure that in the approved fashion of waltzing they will dance themselves out of it.

CHAPTER VIII

OLD ROADS

PRACTICAL inconvenience attends living at the junction of the Is-not and the Is. To make myself better understood, I must explain.

On October 11th, 1809, Colonel Mudge published the Ordnance Survey of the county which I grace with my presence. In that map he entered a Proposed Road, running about four miles from N. to S. through my property, and in front of my house. I was not alive at the time, so the expression "my house" is inexact, it was the house of my grandfather. This proposed road was to be a main artery of traffic, and a county road,—but it was never carried out. To carry it out would have been inconvenient, as the walled garden of the house, with very good jargonelle and Bon-chrétien pears lies athwart the proposed course, and an ancient black fig-tree that produces abundantly every year grows precisely on the site of the proposed road. I presume that my grandfather raised objections. Anyhow the road was never made. However, since the survey of 1809, map-makers—convinced that what was then proposed has been in effect carried out—have systematically entered this road as an accomplished fact.

Now perhaps the reader can understand what it is to live on the point of junction of the Is and Is-not. The road indicated on the maps is not in existence, and yet the public consider, on the authority of the maps, that it is.

Then, again, I live in another way on the Is and Is-not. In 1836 a new and excellent road—now a county road—was carried at right angles to the proposed road, leading into the old high-road about a mile and a half from my house, and connecting that old high-road with the principal market town of the district, about nine miles off. Before this was constructed, the old way ran up hill and down dale in a series of scrambles, straight as an arrow; and one stretch of this road is now utterly impassable, it is simply a water-course, and a torrent rushes down it in a series of cascades over steps of slate-rock in winter, and after rain. Now—will it be believed?—just as the maps have accepted the proposed road as if it had really been made, because it was marked by Col. Mudge, so they have all ignored this main county road, because it did not exist in the days of Col. Mudge, and they persist in giving the old road, and ignoring the new one, that makes a great sweep through valleys, and indeed describes two sides of an obtuse-angled triangle, of which the old road forms the hypothenuse.

Now the reader will understand even more clearly how it is that I live on the what is, yet is not. The road is there—rates are paid to keep it up, and yet—it is not in any map, though it has been in existence for more than half a century.

Now for the practical inconvenience. One day I saw a party of men with guns walking across my grounds, in front of my house. I knew they had been poaching, and so I rushed out after them.

"What are you about? Why are you trespassing?" I roared. One of them pulled out a map and pointed. "We are going along the Queen's highway. Double black edges mark a main road. We cannot be trespassing." I was silenced.

One day I found school-boys in my walled garden eating my Bon-chrétien pears. I ordered them off, threatening them with vengeance.

"Please, sir, we did not know we were doing wrong. On the map we saw that this was a highway, and we thought we were at liberty to take anything that grows on the road." Bad maps and over-education had robbed me of my Bon-chrétien pears.

That is the disadvantage of living on or near the site of a road that is not, but which the authorities that enlighten the minds of the ignorant assert to be. My notion is, that the Press is the great instrument for the diffusion of false information among the masses. Nothing will break that conviction in me. An acquaintance was staying at the market town, and I invited him over to dinner. He hired a trap and drove himself. He had the map, he could manage, he said. He never arrived. Trusting to the map, he had gone by the old road, and had been precipitated down the cascade. The horse had fallen, the trap was smashed, and my friend's hip was dislocated.

So now every one can see that there really is great practical inconvenience in living at the junction of the Is-not yet Is, or the Is and Is-not.

I have a coachman who has been in the family for seventy-five years, and is one of the last surviving representatives of the all-but-extinct race of Caleb Balderstone. This old man remembers the state of the country before most of the new roads were made, before Macadam's system was introduced, and very curious stories he can tell of the old roads, and the travelling thereon. Formerly the roads were—not exactly paved, but made by the thrusting of big stones into holes which they more or less adequately filled. Then on top of all were put smaller stones, picked up from the fields, and not broken at all. As I have got the old road near my gates, for about a mile, closed to all but foot-passengers—though the maps persist in attempting to send carriages over it—I can see exactly what they were. This bit of road is cut between banks eight and nine feet high, has been sawn through soil and rock by the traffic of centuries, assisted by streams of water in winter. The floor is a series of rocky steps, and I can recall when these steps were eased to the traveller by the heaping of boulders on them producing a rude slope. But as with every heavy rain a rush of water went down this road, it dislodged the boulders, and woe betide the horse descending the steep declivity of loosely distributed rolling stones on an irregular and fragile stair of slates.

My great-great-grandmother had a famous black bull. The contemporary Duke of B., who was a fancier of cattle, wanted to buy it, but madam refused to sell. Again he sent over, offering double what he had offered before, but was again refused. Then said the Duke, "Tell madam, that if she will sell me that bull, I will gallop my horse down the road without saddle or bridle." She sent him the bull as a present, without exacting the ride, which would have in all likelihood cost him his life.

In old novels the sinking of the wheel of a chaise in a mud-hole, or the breakage of the carriage, is an ordinary and oft-recurring incident. The wonder to me is, that chaises ever made any progress over these old roads without being splintered to atoms. How was it that china, glass, mirrors, ever reached the country houses intact? I applied to my coachman.

"Well, sir, you see, nothing was carried in waggons then, but on packhorses, that is to say, no perishable goods. My grandfather was a packman. Those were rare times." And he showed me the old packmen's traces, across the woods where now trees grow of fifty years' standing. Indeed, alongside of many modernized roads the old packmen's courses may still be traced. There was great skill required in packing; the packhorse had crooks on its back, and the goods were hung to these crooks. The crooks were formed of two poles, about ten feet long, bent when green into the required curve, and when dried in that shape were connected by horizontal bars. A pair of crooks, thus completed, was slung over the pack-saddle, one swinging on each side, to make the balance true. The short crooks, called crubs, were slung in a similar manner. These were of stouter fabric, and formed an angle; these were used for carrying heavy materials.

I shall doubtless be excused if I quote some old verses written fifty years ago, comparing marriage to a Devonshire lane, but which will equally apply to any old road—

"In a Devonshire lane, as I trotted along
T'other day, much in want of a subject for song,
Thinks I to myself, I have hit on a strain,
Sure Marriage is much like a Devonshire lane.

In the first place 'tis long, and when once you are in it,
It holds you as fast as a cage does a linnet;
For howe'er rough and dirty the road may be found,
Drive forward you must, there is no turning round.

But though 'tis so long, it is not very wide,
For two are the most that together can ride;
And e'en then, 'tis a chance, but they get in a pother,
And jostle and cross and run foul of each other.

Oft Poverty greets them with mendicant looks,
And Care pushes by them, o'er-laden with crooks;
And Strife's grazing wheels try between them to pass,
And Stubbornness blocks up the way on her ass.

Then the banks are so high, to the left hand and right,
That they shut out the beauties around them from sight;
And hence you'll allow, 'tis an inference plain,
That Marriage is just like a Devonshire lane!

But thinks I too, these banks, within which we are pent,
With bud, blossom, and berry are richly besprent;
And the conjugal fence, which forbids us to roam,
Looks lovely when decked with the comforts of home.

In the rock's gloomy crevice the bright holly grows;
The ivy waves fresh o'er the withering rose,
And the evergreen love of a virtuous wife
Soothes the roughness of care,—cheers the winter of life.

Then long be the journey, and narrow the way,
I'll rejoice that I've seldom a turnpike to pay;
And whate'er others say, be the last to complain,
Though Marriage be just like a Devonshire lane."

"Ah, sir!" said my old coachman, "them was jolly times. The packmen used to travel in a lot together, and when they put up at an inn for the night, there was fun;—not but what they was a bit rough-like. I mind when one day they found a jackass straying, and didn't know whose it was, nor didn't ask either. They cut handfuls of rushes, and with cords they swaddled the ass up with rushes, and then set alight to him. Well, sir, that ass ran blazing like a fireball for four miles before he dropped. Them was jolly times."

"Not for asses, Caleb?"

"Certainly not for asses."

"But why did the packmen travel together, Caleb?"

"Well, sir, you see, packmen at times carried a lot o' money about with them; and it did happen now and then that lonely packmen were robbed and murdered."

"Then hardly jolly times for packmen?"

"Well, I don't know," answered Balderstone, drawing his hand and whip across his mouth. "There was packmen then, and perhaps just here and there one got murdered; but now they are all put out of the way, which is worst of all."

After a little consideration Caleb went on—"Now, I mind a curious circumstance that happened when I was a young man, just about sixty years ago. At that time there were no shops about, and once or twice in the year I was sent with a waggon and a team up to the county town (thirty-five miles off) to bring down groceries and all sorts o' things for the year. I used to start at four in the morning. One autumn morning I had started before daybreak, and I lay in the covered waggon, and the two horses they knew the road and went on. But all at once both halted, and though I cracked my whip they would not stir. I got out with the lantern, and saw that they were all of a tremble, both with their heads down looking at something, apparently, in the road. I moved the lantern about, but could see nothing in the road, and then I coaxed the horses, but they would not stir a step; then I whipped them. All at once both together gave a leap into the air, just as if they were leaping a gate, and away they dashed along the road for a mile afore I could stop them, and then they were sweating as if they had been raced in a steeplechase, and covered with foam, and trembling still. Now I was away two days, and on the third I came back, and the curious thing is—when I came back I heard that a packer had been robbed and murdered whilst I was away at that very spot, and where my horses had leaped it was over the exact place where the dead man was found lying twenty-four hours later. If they'd jumped after the murder I'd have thought nothing of it, but they jumped before the man was killed."

Road-making was formerly intrusted to the parochial authorities, and there was no supervision. It was carried out in slovenly and always in an unsystematic manner. In adopting a direct or circuitous line of way, innumerable predilections interfered, and parishes not infrequently quarrelled about the roads. The dispute between broad and narrow gauges raged long before railway lines were laid. A market town and a seaport would naturally desire to have ample verge and room enough on their highways for the transport of grain and other commodities from the interior, and for carriage of manufactured goods, or importations to the interior. On the other hand, isolated parishes would contend that driftways sufficed for their demands, and that they could house their crops, or bring their flour from the mill through the same ruts which had served their forefathers.

After the Civil Wars an impetus was given to road-making; an Act was passed authorizing a small toll to pay for the maintenance of the highways. The turnpike gate was originally a bar supported on two posts on the opposite sides of the road, and the collector sat in the open air at his seat of custom. I remember fifty years ago travelling in Germany, where at the toll-gate was a little house; one end of the bar was heavily weighted, the other fastened by a chain that led into the turnpike man's room. The toll-man thrust forth a pole with a bag at the end, into which the coin was put, he drew in the bag at his window, unhooked the chain, and the weight sent the bar flying up, the carriage passed under, and then the bar was pulled down again.

The people did not see the advantage of the toll-bar when first introduced, and riots broke out. The road surveyor was mobbed and beaten, the toll-bar was torn away and burnt. Even with systematic mending, the old roads were bad, for the true principle on which roads should be made was not known. John Loudon MacAdam, born 1756, died 1836, was the first to draw attention to the proper mode of road-making. He was an American, of Scottish descent. In 1819 he published A Practical Essay on the Scientific Repair and Preservation of Public Roads, and in 1820, Remarks on the Present State of Road-making. How little science was thought to have to do with the roads may be judged from the fact, that under the heading of Roads, the old Encyclopædia Britannica of 1797 has not a word to say. "Road-making!" one may suppose a surveyor of that period to have said, "any fool can make a road. If one finds a hole anywhere, clap a stone into it."

I have walked over the St. Gotthard Pass, and there we have the old road traceable in many places, and we can compare it with the new road. The old one was paved here and there rudely. Some of our old English roads were likewise paved. MacAdam's principle was this. Make all roads with the highest point in the middle, then the water runs off it, instead of—as in the old roads—lodging in the middle. Next, do not pave the road at all, but lay in a bottom—metal it—with broken stones, to the depth of six or eight inches, and then cover these with another layer, broken smaller, to the depth of two or three inches. Then all will be welded together into a compact and smooth mass. MacAdam originally proposed that the small upper coat of stones should be laid on in a corduroy fashion across the road, but this was abandoned for an uniform covering, as more speedily applied, and more effective.

What a time people took formerly in travelling over old roads! There is a house just two miles distant from mine, by the new unmapped road. Before 1837, when that road was made, it was reached in so circuitous a manner, and by such bad lanes, and across an unbridged river, that my grandfather and his family when they dined with our neighbours, two miles off, always spent the night at their house.

In 1762, a rich gentleman, who had lived in a house of business in Lisbon, and had made his fortune, returned to England, and resolved to revisit his paternal home in Norfolk. His wish was further stimulated by the circumstance that his sister and sole surviving relative dwelt beside one of the great broads, where he thought he might combine some shooting with the pleasure of renewing his friendships of childhood. From London to Norwich his way was tolerably smooth and prosperous, and by the aid of a mail coach he performed the journey in three days. But now commenced his difficulties. Between the capital and his sister's dwelling lay twenty miles of country roads. He ordered a coach and six, and set forth on his fraternal quest. The six hired horses, although of strong Flanders breed, were soon engulfed in a black miry pool, his coach followed, and the merchant was dragged out of the window by two cowherds, and mounted on one of the wheelers; he was brought back to Norwich, and nothing could ever induce him to resume the search for his sister, and to revisit his ancestral home.

The death of good Queen Bess was not known in some of the remoter parishes of Devon and in Cornwall until the court mourning for her had been laid aside; and in the churches of Orkney prayers were put up for King James II. three months after he had abdicated.

"However," I asked of Caleb, "could the huge masses of granite have been moved that form the pillars in the church, and the gate-posts, and the fireplace in the hall?"

"Well, sir, on truckamucks."

"Truckamucks!"

"In the old times they didn't have wheels, but a sort of cart with the ends of the shafts carried out behind and dragging on the ground. In fact, the cart was nothing but two young trees, and the roots dragged, and the tops were fastened to the horse. When they wanted to move a heavy weight they used four trees, and lashed the middle ones together."

"No carts or waggons, then?"

"Only one waggon in the parish, and that your grandfather's, and that could travel only on the high-road. Not many other conveyances either."

It is a marvel to us how the old china and glass travelled in those days; but the packer was a man of infinite care and skill in the management of fragile wares.

Does the reader remember the time when all such goods were brought by carriers? How often they got broken if intrusted to the stage-coaches, how rarely if they came by the carrier. The carrier's waggon was securely packed, and time was of no object to the driver, he went very slowly and very carefully over bad ground. The carrier's life was a very jolly one, and few songs were more popular in the west of England than that of The Jolly Waggoner—

"When first I went a-waggoning, a-waggoning did go,
I filled my parents' hearts with sorrow, trouble, grief, and woe;
And many are the hardships too, that since I have gone through.
Sing Wo! my lads, sing wo!
Drive on, my lads, heigh-ho!
Who would not live the life of the jolly waggoner?

It is a cold and stormy night, and I'm wet to the skin,
I'll bear it with contentment till I get to the inn,
And then I'll sit a-drinking with the landlord and his kin.
Sing Wo! &c.

Now summer is a-coming on—what pleasure we shall see!
The small birds blithely singing, so sweet on every tree,
The blackbirds and the thrushes, too, are whistling merrily.
Sing Wo! &c.

Now Michaelmas is coming—what pleasure we shall find!
'Twill make the gold to fly, my lads, like chaff before the wind,
And every lad shall kiss his lass, so loving and so kind.
Sing Wo! &c."

Since the introduction of steam two additional verses have been added to this song—

"Along the country roads, alas! but waggons few are seen,
The world is topsy-turvy turned, and all things go by steam,
And all the past is passed away, like to a morning dream.
Sing Wo! &c.

The landlords cry, What shall we do? our business is no more,
The railroad it has ruined us, who badly fared before;
'Tis luck and gold to one or two, but ruined are a score.
Sing Wo! &c."

The leathern belt worn by the groom nowadays is the survival of the strap to which the lady held, as she sat on a pillion behind her groom. The horses ridden in those days must have been strong, or the distances not considerable, and the pace moderate, for to carry two full-grown persons cannot have been a trifle for a horse on bad roads.

"It is of some importance," said Sydney Smith, "at what period a man is born. A young man alive at this period hardly knows to what improvements of human life he has been introduced; and I would bring before his notice the changes that have taken place in England since I began to breathe the breath of life—a period of seventy years. I have been nine hours sailing from Dover to Calais before the invention of steam. It took me nine hours to go from Taunton to Bath before the invention of railroads. In going from Taunton to Bath I suffered between ten thousand and twelve thousand severe contusions before stone-breaking MacAdam was born. I paid fifteen pounds in a single year for repair of carriage-springs on the pavement of London, and I now glide without noise or fracture on wooden pavement. I can walk without molestation from one end of London to another; or, if tired, get into a cheap and active cab, instead of those cottages on wheels which the hackney coaches were at the beginning of my life. I forgot to add, that as the basket of the stage-coaches in which luggage was then carried had no springs, your clothes were rubbed all to pieces; and that even in the best society, one-third of the gentlemen were always drunk. I am now ashamed that I was not formerly more discontented, and am utterly surprised that all these changes and inventions did not occur two centuries ago."

CHAPTER IX

FAMILY PORTRAITS

ONE day a very grand and, as she conceived, original idea came into my grandmothers head. She was resolved to represent pictorially, on a sheet of cartridge-paper, all the confluent streams of blood in her children's veins, of the families to which they were entitled to draw blood through past alliances.

So my grandmother got out her ruler and colour-box, and a pallet and brushes, and filled a little glass with water. Presently a pedigree was drawn out by the aid of compasses and a parallel ruler. Then she rubbed her paints and set to work colouring. She dabbed some vermilion on Father A, and gamboge on Mother B; then on the next in the same generation, Father C, she put sage-green; and his wife, Mother D, she indicated with Prussian blue. The son of vermilion A and gamboge B was R. That was simple enough; in his arteries flowed a vivid tide of combined vermilion and gamboge. He married S, who was the offspring of sage-green C and Prussian blue D; consequently her arteries were flowing with rather a dingy mixture of sage-green and Prussian blue. Now R and S had a child, P, and his veins were charged with a combination of vermilion and gamboge and sage-green and Prussian blue.

When my grandmother had got so far, she bit the end of her paint-brush; for P, who was her husband's father, of course married, and her mother-in-law must be also represented by a combination of four colours. She took the end of the brush out of her mouth and rubbed emerald green and carmine. E and F should symbolize her husband's mother's grandparents. E brought into the family a stream of carmine blood, and F one of vivid emerald. Then the veins of her step-mother represented a mixed tide of carmine and emerald and of two other families, as yet unindicated. To these she promptly appropriated violet and orange. Now at last was she able to tabulate the constituents of her husband's blood; it was composed of minute rills of vermilion, gamboge, sage-green, Prussian blue, carmine, emerald green, violet, and orange. Already she had trenched on the composite colours. Now a great dismay fell on my grandmother; for she had to complete the same process for the exemplification of her own blood; and for her ancestry not only were no primary colours left, but even no secondary. She had to represent them with brown, lavender, slate,—yes, oh joy! there was another blue, cobalt!—verdegris, lemon yellow, black, and white. She hesitated some while before employing the verdegris. She never completed that table; for she was aghast at the rivers of mud, literal mud, which, according to her scheme, flowed through the arteries of her offspring. Now look at this table. Consider, it is only one of a pedigree through five generations.

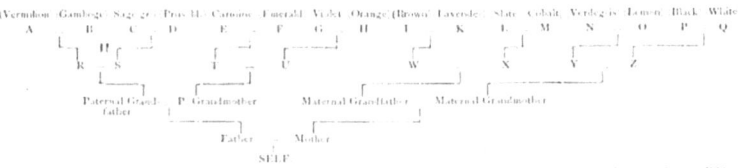

Every one of my readers, every human being, nay, every beast, and bird, and fish, and reptile, represents the 16 ancestors of four generations, that means 32 independent streams of blood in the fifth generation, and 1004 currents in the tenth generation, and 32,128 rivulets of distinct blood in the fifteenth generation, and 1,028,096, if we go back to the twentieth generation. Take thirty years as a generation, then, in the reign of Henry III., there were over a million independent individuals, walking, talking, eating, marrying, whose united blood was to be, in 1889, blended in your veins. Why, that ogre of a sailor in the Bab Ballads, who represented a whole ship's crew, because, when shipwrecked, he had eaten them, is nothing to you. The whole population of London, of Middlesex, was not a million, then. You represent a large county—Yorkshire, for instance.

Our arteries are very sluices, through which an incredible amount of confluent rills unite to rush, the drainage of the whole social country-side.

Such being the case, does it not seem a farce to talk about family types, and family likenesses, and family peculiarities beyond one or two generations at most? And yet it is not a farce; for what comes out abundantly clear is, that certain streams are stronger than others, and colour and affect for several generations the quality of the blood with which they mingle. Not so only, but earlier types reappear after the lapse of time as distinct as though there had been no intermediate blood mixture, as though there had been filiation by gemmation, as is the case with sponges.

One day I was visiting a friend, when I was struck by the excellence of a portrait in his hall of a very refined and beautiful old lady; there was nothing characteristic in the dress. Being a fancier in portraiture, and being mightily ill-contented with modern portrait-painting, this picture pleased me especially; it was a picture as well as a portrait, harmonious in colour and tone, and artistically focussed. Moreover, it was a perfectly life-like "presentiment" of my friend's wife. He and she were both old people. Said I to my friend, "What an admirable likeness! The artist has not only made a good picture, but he has caught your wife's expression as well as features and peculiar colouring. Who is the painter? I did not know we had the man nowadays who could have painted such a portrait."

"Oh," he answered, "that is not my wife—it is her great-grandmother."

Thus the wife represented four united streams of two generations back, but she represented in face, and represented exactly, only one of them.

Now for another instance. In a certain family that I know intimately, a son and a female cousin are as much alike as though they were twin brother and sister; what is the more remarkable is, that they deviate altogether from the type of their brothers and sisters, parents, uncles, and aunts. But, and here is the curious fact, they resemble, even ludicrously, an ancestor whose miniature and portrait in oils are in the possession of the family. I draw out the pedigree. I must premise that the portrait is of a gentleman in forget-me-not blue velvet, and he goes in the family by the name of the Blue Man.

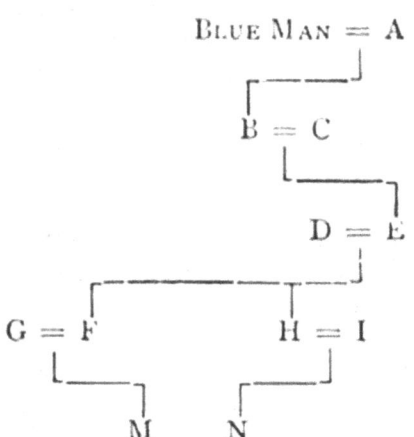

M and N are the cousins, male and female, who are as alike as twins, and they are exact reproductions of the Blue Man, notwithstanding that through C, D, G, and I come in fresh streams of blood, that two entirely independent rivers flush the veins of M and N respectively, coming in from G and I. They have the blood of C and D in common, but alike disregard their qualities; so also do they reject the blood of their respective mothers, and go back to a common ancestor in the reign of Queen Anne.

But I can give a still more remarkable instance of atavism, which also must be illustrated by a table. Here the likeness goes back even further, and, like that above, also through the maternal line.

There is in the same old manor-house as that in which hangs the Blue Man another picture, painted by Carlo Maratti, in or about 1672, of a certain Sir Edward, a dandy, in long flowing curls, a beautiful Steenkirk, a cherry ribbon round his neck, and also about his wrists. The face is fine, haughty, somewhat dreamy. It was painted of him when he was a young man of about five-and-twenty. Hanging near him is his elder brother, also with flowing hair, a bluff, good-natured man in appearance, quite different in character from the knight, one may judge, and certainly not like him in feature. Now the knight, Sir Edward, died without issue, and left all his property to his great-nephew, the grandson of his elder brother James. That nephew bought estates in Nottinghamshire, and for two hundred years the family he founded has been apart from the elder branch, which lives in the west of England, and which owns the picture.

One day recently there came into the neighbourhood a descendant of James, and calling at the house of his kinsman, unconsciously seated himself beneath the picture of Sir Edward. He was a young man of about four-and-twenty. He was at once greeted with an exclamation of astonishment and amusement. He was extraordinarily like the portrait; had he but been dressed in stamped black velvet, worn curls, a Steenkirk, and cherry ribbons, he might have been the same man. Now look at this pedigree, and note the remarkable fact. He did not hail from the knight, whom he resembled, but from his brother James, whom he did not resemble. The knight, Sir Edward, must therefore have inherited the features of an earlier ancestor, who was also, of course, the ancestor of his brother; so that this young man in 1888 bore the face and features of a still earlier member of the family, whose likeness has not been preserved, if it were ever taken. Here is a family likeness going back six or seven generations. We cannot be certain that the characteristic features of Sir Edward were derived from his father or his mother. Nor is this likeness found only in N. It exists also in his father L, though not in so strong a degree, or, at all events, it is less apparent in an old man of sixty than in a young man of four-and-twenty. Curiously enough, the portrait of Elizabeth, the ancestress through whom these two, L and N, derive their likeness to Sir Edward, shows none of these characteristics. They remained latent in her, but reappeared in her grandson and great-grandson. Unfortunately the pictures of D and F, who intervened, have not been preserved, or their whereabouts have not been discovered, so that it is not possible to track the likeness through two generations that intervene between Elizabeth in 1780 and James in 1680.

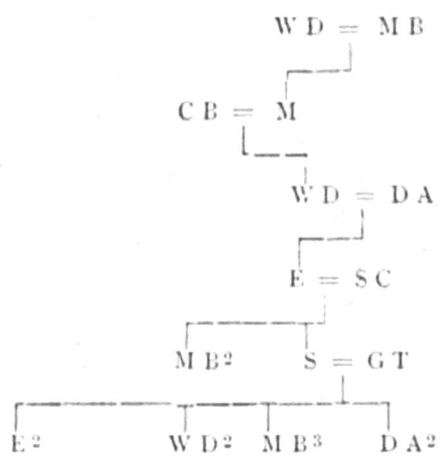

It has been conjectured that a child sitting daily in the presence of a certain portrait insensibly assumes a likeness to it; but such a conjecture will not satisfy the case just mentioned, for L and N till recently had never seen the picture which they so closely resembled.

There is another point connected with family portraits that has given me occasion of thought and speculation; and that is, the way in which those children who are named after an ancestor or ancestress sometimes, I do not say often or always, but certainly sometimes, do in a very remarkable manner receive the stamp of the features of that ancestor after whom named. This has nothing to do with the naming of the child at baptism because of a supposed resemblance, for in very young infants none such can be traced, but the likeness grows in the child to the person whose name it bears.

Now here is a bit of pedigree, with the likenesses that exist curiously agreeing with the Christian names. In this relation of a new generation to an old there is a point to be remarked. E2 is in character, in manner, and in tastes and pursuits exactly what E was, but does not resemble him in face. W D2 is just like W D, his great-great-great-grandfather, whose double Christian name he bears. M B2 and M B3 are like M B in face, and M B2 resembles her great-great-grandmother in face and in character. D A2 is absurdly like her great-grandmother, whose double name she bears, but is as yet too young for the mental characteristics to show themselves, or at all events to have become sufficiently emphasized to enable one to say whether, in mind as in face, she resembles her great-grandmother.

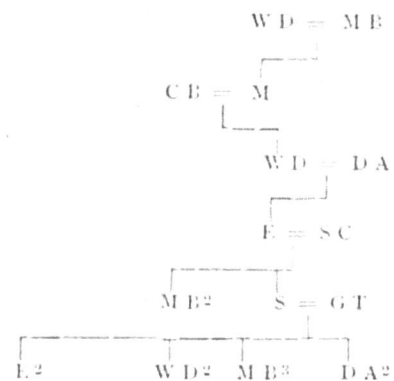

Now this may be accidental, but if so, it is a very curious and remarkable accident. Noticing it in other cases, I have sometimes wondered whether there may be in it more than accident. The old Norsemen believed that by calling a child after a certain great man, some of that great man's luck and spiritual force passed with his name to the child. The idea among Roman Catholic parents of giving their offspring the names of saints is, that they put the children under the special patronage, influence, and tutelage of the saint after whom they are called. Now—is there in these ideas anything more than a fancy, a delusion, a superstition? Is it possible that a mysterious effluence should pass from the spirit of the departed to the child that reproduces his or her name, and that this effluence should affect, modify, and impress the features and character of the child?

It is remarkable the way in which tricks perpetuate themselves. I know some one who, when a boy, had to be broken of the absurd habit of slapping the sole of his right boot with his right hand every now and then behind his back, as he walked. An old aunt saw him do this one day, and she said, "How odd! we had a world of trouble with his father when he was a child—about this very thing."

I may, in connection with this, mention a personal matter. My paternal grandfather's sister, Jacquetta Baring, married Sir Stafford Northcote, in 1791; she was the grandmother of the late Lord Iddesleigh, who was, accordingly, my cousin, but whom I never met. One day I was with one of his sons, who, whilst in conversation with me, laughed, and then said, "Excuse me, but there are many little ways you have, both of turn of the head and movements of the hand, that bring my father continually before my mind whilst you are speaking with me."

These little tricks of manner are therefore not personal, are not the result of association and imitation, but travel through the blood.

But to return to family portraits. That, in spite of the influx of fresh blood from all quarters, a certain family type remains, one can hardly doubt in looking through a genuine series of family pictures. I knew a case of an artist who had been employed in a certain house, where he had become familiar with the family portraits, which he had cleaned, relined and restored. Some of the early pictures of the family had been lost, in fact sold, by a spendthrift—another Charles Surface—who did not shrink from disposing of his mother's picture by Sir Joshua Reynolds. The head of the family knew where some two or three of these pictures had gone; they had been bought by a family akin to his, and the representative of that family very kindly acceded to his request that he might have them copied. The artist was sent to that gentleman's house to do what was desired. He was introduced into the dining-room, where hung over a score of portraits, but he went directly to the two which belonged to the family whose paintings he had cleaned, singled them out from the rest, and said, "These I am sure belong to the X—s. I know the type of face." He was right; he had spotted the only two which were not pictures of the A family, but were of the family X.

The delight of watching the re-emergence of a disappeared family likeness, as generations pass, is, no doubt, the chief delight of having a good series of family pictures. But there is an advantage in such a series which is not perhaps much considered, and that is the linking of the present generation in thought with the past. Since, with the Reformation, prayer for the dead ceased, our association with the world of the departed has fallen into total disregard, and we neither think of holding any communion of thought and good-will with our forebears, nor suppose that they can entertain any kindly thought of and wishes for us and our welfare. And yet, how much we owe them! Our beautiful estates, our dear old houses, the laying out of the parks and grounds, the cutting of the terraces, the digging of the ponds, the planting of the stately trees, the gathering together of our plate, our books, our pictures, our old furniture. Nay, more, if we have not inherited these, we have from them some twists in our mind, some terms in our speech, some physical or psychical characteristics, some virtues and some faults.

We owe to those old people more than we suppose. To their self-restraint, their guileless walk, their frugal ways, we owe our own hale bodies and strict consciences. Consider what misery a strain of tainted blood brings into a family—a strain of blood that carries vicious propensities with it. Well, if we have good in us, if we are scrupulous, honest, truthful, self-controlled, it comes to us in a large measure along with our pure blood from honest ancestry.

How can we sit in the beautiful halls and panelled boudoirs of the old people, and not be thankful to them for having made them so charming? How can we walk in the avenues they planted, pick the flowering shrubs they grouped and bedded, and not be grateful to them?

To plant a tree is a most unselfish work, for very few men live to see the trees they have planted reach such a size as to give pleasure to themselves. Men plant for their sons and grandsons; and their sons and grandsons who enjoy these trees should think for a moment of those to whose forethought they owe them. I confess I like, when I have enjoyed the beauty of some avenue, or clump of stately trees, to look at the picture of the planter of them, and say, "Thank you, dear old man, for the pleasure you have given to me, and will give to my children after me."

We have something yet to learn from the Chinese. The only religion of the Celestials is the worship of their ancestors. Every race probably inherits some truth that it can and is destined to impart to the world. The Chinese lack the deeper vision which can look up to the great Father of spirits above, but yet from them we may acquire thought of and love for our forebears.

> "They are all gone into a world of light,
> And I alone sit lingering here!
> Their very memory is fair and bright,
> And my sad thoughts does clear.
> It glows and glitters in my cloudy breast,
> Like stars upon some gloomy grove;
> Or those faint beams in which this hill is dressed
> After the sun's remove."

So sang Vaughan, a poet of the Restoration; and if one attempts it one can feel with him, that it is a pleasure and a rest to think of, and cultivate affection for, those of our family who belong to the past.

In many an old mansion the story goes that an ancestor or ancestress walks there, is to be seen occasionally between the glimpses of the moon visiting the old house, and generally as foretoken of some event intimately concerning the family. Such a story is common enough. We think that possibly these ancient ghosts may reappear to acquaint themselves how we are getting on, but it never occurs to us to visit them, and walk in spirit their desolate region, and cheer them with a kindly expression, and a word of good-will. Well, I think that a set of family portraits does help one to that, does link us somehow to these dead forefathers, and serves as a vehicle of mental communication between us.

Then, again, the family scamp is of use. We had one in our family. I am thankful to say we do not inherit his wild blood, as he died unmarried. He sold the bulk of the ancestral estates, and got rid of everything he could get rid of. But then—since his death he has stood as a warning to each successive generation. The children go before his picture and hear the story of his misdeeds, and it sinks into their hearts, and they learn frugality. They go over the acres that would have been theirs, but for the scamp; they see the old mansion, a quadrangle, which they would have had a dance about, had it not been for the scamp; they know that there are gaps in the series of family portraiture, because the pictures were sold by the scamp; and so they grow up with great fear in their minds lest they also should by any chance be even as he; and so the scamp is of good after all.

CHAPTER X

THE VILLAGE MUSICIAN

THE press and the railway are sweeping away all the old individualities and peculiarities that marked the country. It has been said, and said truly, that the railway has abolished everywhere in Europe a local cuisine, so that the traveller, whether in England, France, in Italy, Russia, at Constantinople, and even at Cairo, has the same menu at table-d'hôte. There was a time when, by travelling, you could pick up culinary ideas. That time is now past. You find exactly the same dishes, served in the same order, everywhere; and when fowl and salad come on, you know everywhere that the meat courses have arrived at their full stop. Costumes also are disappearing everywhere, no men now wear them, hardly any women, except a few artists' models on the steps of the Trinità at Rome, and a few German tourists who dress up like mountaineers when excursioning among the Tyrolean Alps.

It is said that the Chinese all dress alike, think alike, talk alike, act alike, eat the same food, take the same amusements, and look alike. Civilization is making us all Chinese, we are losing our individuality and our independence, and, it must be admitted, casting away behind us what constituted the picturesqueness and variety of life.

In the old times in country places, away from towns, there was much that was of interest; men and women had then quaint ways, stood out as characters, and impressed themselves on those who were around them. Now, all are afraid of being peculiar, of not being like every one else, of using a word, doing an act, thinking a thought which has not the sanction of—vulgarity, in the true acceptation of the term, according to its derivation—of being common.

One looks back, with a little compunction, on those old times. There was a freshness and charm about them which can never be recovered. Every one in a village knew every one else, and all his belongings; every one was related, and a stranger from a few miles off passed as a foreigner. To "go foreign" was to leave the parish. This was, of course, carried to extraordinary lengths in some places, and neighbouring villages regarded each other with traditional jealousy. This was not commendable. There is a story told of two villages, one called Mary Tavy, the adjoining called Peter Tavy, that is to say, St. Mary on the Tavy and St. Peter on the Tavy, on the borders of Dartmoor, that regarded each other for ages with animosity. One day after a storm of rain the river Tavy rolled down volumes of water, and a poor wretch was caught by the flood on a rock in mid-stream; he was unable to reach the bank. He screamed for assistance. Presently a man came along the side and halted, and called to the fellow in danger, "I say, be you a Peter Tavy or a Mary Tavy man?" "Peter Tavy," answered the wretch in danger. "Throw me a rope, or I shall be drownded." "No, no," answered he on the land, "I be a Mary Tavy man; so go on hollering till a Peter Tavy chap comes by;" and he left the fellow in distress to his fate.

This exclusiveness had its bad side, but it had its redeeming side also. There can be no question that the force of popular feeling, the sense of relationship, the feeling of belonging to a certain village, or class, did act as a strong moral support to many a young man and woman. They felt that they dared not bring disgrace on their whole class, or village, by misconduct. The sense of belonging to, being one member of a community, in which, if one member were honoured, all the members rejoiced with it, and if one were disgraced, the humiliation fell on all, was very strong and tough. That is to an immense extent gone, and can never be restored. We are all cosmopolitan now, and live and die to ourselves.

But let us come to some of the peculiar features of old village life, before there were railways, and when the post did not come every day.

At that time most villages had their feasts, revels, harvest homes, ringers' suppers, shearing feasts, and other entertainments. Some of us can remember when in the village churches the gallery was occupied by the village band, fiddles and viol, ophicleide, flute &c. They were done away with, and the hand-organ took its place in some churches, a real organ or a harmonium in others. It was a sad mistake of the clergy to try to abolish the old orchestra;—no doubt the playing was not very good, and the instruments were out of tune; no doubt also there was much quarrelling and little harmony among the performers, but an institution should be improved, not abolished. That gave the death-blow to instrumental music in our villages. Previously the smallest village had its half-dozen men who could play on some instruments. Now you find that there are half a dozen boys who can manage the concertina—that is all.

These instrumentalists attended all the festivities in a village, wakes, harvest homes, revels, and weddings, and were well received and well treated. They played old country dances, old ballads, old concerted pieces of no ordinary merit. In some parish chests may be found volumes of rudely written music, which belonged to these performers, mostly sacred, but not always so.

When in 1617 James I. was making a progress through Lancashire, he found that the Puritan magistrates had prohibited and unlawfully punished the people for using their "lawful recreations and honest exercises" on holidays; and next year he issued a declaration concerning sports and merry-makings, such as May-games, morris-dances, Whitsun-ales, the setting up of maypoles; and James very wisely said, "If these be taken away from the meaner sort, who labour hard all the week, they will have no recreations at all to refresh their spirits; and in place thereof it will set up filthy tipplings and drunkenness, and breed a number of idle and discontented speeches in their ale-houses." Also it would "hinder the conversion of many, whom their priests will take occasion hereby to vex, persuading them that no honest mirth or recreation is lawfully tolerable in our religion."

At the present day we hardly realize the extent to which music was cultivated in old times, so that England—not Italy, Germany, or France—was the great musical nation of Europe. What astonished foreigners, when they visited England in the reign of Henry VIII. and Elizabeth, was the perfection to which music was brought here, and the widespread knowledge of music that prevailed. France had its music school created by Sully, a Florentine by birth, who was placed at the head of a band of violins by Louis XIV. At that time "not half the musicians of France were able to play at sight." Even that band, got together with difficulty, could play nothing at sight. Nor did Sully effect any great reform in this respect, for when the Regent, Duke of Orleans, wished to hear Corelli's sonatas, which were newly brought from Rome, no three persons were to be found in Paris who could play them, and he was obliged to content himself with having them sung to him by three voices. On the other hand, in England at that time every gentleman was expected to be able either to sing a part at sight, or play a part on some instrument or other. As a regular thing after supper, the party in a country house adjourned to the music-room, and there spent the rest of the evening in singing or in instrumental music. Nor was this knowledge of music confined to the upper classes. A curious instance of this we find in Pepys' diary. That diary extends between the years 1660-1669. In the course of his diary, four maids are mentioned as being in his household, to attend on his wife, and a boy who waited on himself. All of these seem to have possessed, as an ordinary qualification, some musical skill and knowledge. Of the first of the serving-maids he says (November 17, 1662), "After dinner, talking with my wife, and making Mrs. Gosnell (the maid) sing—I am mightily pleased with her humour and singing." And again, on December 5, "She sings exceedingly well." Within a few months Gosnell was succeeded by Mary Ashwell; and he tells us in March, "I heard Ashwell play first upon the harpsicon, and I find she do play pretty well. Then home by coach, buying at the Temple the printed virginal book for her." The harpsicon and the virginal were the pianofortes of the period, something like square pianos; in the virginal the strings were struck by quills. Of the third maid Mrs. Pepys had, Mary Mercer, he says on September 9, 1664, that she was "a pretty, modest, quiet maid. After dinner my wife and Mercer, Tom (the boy) and I, sat till eleven at night, singing and fiddling, and a great joy it is to see me master of so much pleasure in my house. The girle (Mercer) plays pretty well upon the harpsicon, but only ordinary tunes, but hath a good hand; sings a little, but hath a good voyce and eare. My boy, a brave boy, sings finely, and is the most pleasant boy at present, while his ignorant boy's tricks last, that ever I see." After some time Mercer went to see her mother, and Mrs. Pepys, finding her absent without leave, went after her, found her in her mother's house, and there beat her. The mother having urged that Mary was "not a common prentice girl," and therefore ought not to have been thus chastized, Mrs. Pepys construed it into a question of her right to inflict corporal chastisement, and dismissed Mary.

In October, 1666, says Pepys, "my wife brought a new girle. She is wretched poor, and but ordinary favoured, and we fain to lay out seven or eight pounds worth of clothes upon her back: and I do not think I can esteem her as I could have done another, that had come fine and handsome; and, which is more, her voice, through want of use, is so furred that it do not at present please me; but her manner of singing is such that I shall, I think, take great pleasure in it."

After a while Mary Mercer was taken back, and then we hear of singing on the water, especially after a trip to Greenwich when returning by moonlight. The boy Tom was usually of the party. Of him Pepys says (Oct. 25, 1664), "My boy could not sleep, but wakes about four in the morning, and in bed laying playing on his lute till daylight, and it seems did the like last night, till twelve o'clock." And again, Dec. 26, 1668, "After supper I made the boy play upon his lute, and so, my mind is mighty content,—to bed."

We do not in the least suppose that Pepys' household was singular in the respect of having a succession of musical servants. All people in those times were musical—men, boys, women, and girls, of all classes and degrees. At the fire of London in 1666, Pepys, who was an eye-witness, tells us that the Thames was full of lighters and boats taking in goods, and that he "observed that hardly one lighter or boat in three, that had the goods of a house, but there was a pair of virginals in it."

How those old fellows loved and cared for their instruments! Mace, a writer of 1676, tells how a lute should be treated. "You shall do well," he writes, "even when you lay it by in the day-time, to put it into a bed that is constantly used, between the rug and the blanket, but never between the sheets, because they may be moist. There are great commodities (advantages) in so doing; it will save the strings from breaking; it will keep your lute in good order." He enumerates six conveniences of so doing. At that time a lute, a good one, cost about £100.

So completely was it a matter of course to have music after supper, that Cromwell, a lover of music, only altered the character of the performance. When the ambassadors of Holland came to him, as Lord Protector, on the occasion of peace between the two Commonwealths, after having entertained them at a repast, he and the "Lady Protectrice" led them into the music-hall, where they had a psalm sung. This was in 1654. The dissolution of the cathedral choirs, the abolition of sacred music in the churches, scattered professional musicians over the country. There is a very curious traditional song relative to this change, sung in Devonshire, and called Brixham Town.

It relates how—

> "In Brixham town so rare
> For singing sweet and fair,
> With none that may compair."

The instrumentalists and singers considered that they were the best anywhere. But—

> "There came a man to our town,
> A man of office and in gown,
> Strove to put music down,
> Which most men do adore."

Then the story goes on to exhort him and all others who love not music—

> "Go search out Holy Writ,
> And you will find in it,
> That it is right and fit

To praise the Lord.
On cymbal and with lute,
On organ and with flute,
And voices sweet that suit
All in accord."

Very pointedly the song goes on to mention how an evil spirit haunted Saul, and how it proved that this devil also hated music, and how that when David played on his harp the evil spirit fled. The song ends—

"So now, my friends, adieu;
I hope that all of you
Will pull most just and true
In serving the Lord.
God grant that all of we,
Like angels may agree,
Singing in harmony,
And sweet concord."

There was a great effort made at the time of the Commonwealth to put down all kinds of music. In 1648 the Provost-marshal was given power to arrest all ballad-singers. Organs were everywhere destroyed, and probably a great many viols, lutes, and other instruments. One gentleman, when he adopted Puritanism, had a deep hole dug in his garden, and buried in it "£200 worth of music-books, six feet underground, being, as he said, love-songs and vanity." This was a considerable sum indeed for an amateur to have spent in books of vocal music only; and as he continued to play "psalms and religious hymns on the theorbo," it may be presumed that what was interred formed but a portion of his musical collection.

The singers and instrumentalists dispersed by the orders of Parliament were reduced to the greatest poverty, and went round the country taking up their abode in gentlemen's houses, where they were gladly given quarters, when these gentlemen could afford it; but as many were utterly impoverished, often the musicians frequented the ale-houses, and picked up a precarious subsistence from the tavern frequenters. This had one advantage, for it no doubt helped to educate the village people generally in music. But even thus they got into trouble, for Oliver Cromwell's third Parliament passed an Act ordering the arrest and punishment of all minstrels and musicians who performed in taverns. Hitherto in country places the only instruments used had been rude, and the only music known was the ballad air, which also served as a dance-tune. Hence most of our old dances are known by the names of the ballads to which they were sung. But the dispersion of the orchestras from cathedrals and theatres and large town churches throughout the country places not only brought in a new notion of music, the playing of concerted pieces, but also in a great many cases placed the costly instruments at the disposal of village musicians. The old instrumentalists were obliged to part with their lutes and theorbos, their viol de gambas and violins, at a low price; or dying in the villages where they had settled, they left their loved instruments to such men in the place as seemed likely to make good use of them. These old musicians in country places gathered men about them in their lodgings in the village ale-houses, and taught them a more artistic method of playing, and a higher class of music, and they really gave that impetus to orchestral church music which only died out—shall we not rather say was killed?—within the memory of man.

The old village musician was a man remarkable in his way. One, David Turton, of Horbury, in Yorkshire, was perhaps typical of the better class. A man of intense enthusiasm for his art, and passionate love of his viol; one may be quite sure that his viol shared his bed, taking it by day when Turton was out of it, like Box and Cox. The story was told of him, that he was returning one night from a concert at Wakefield, where he had been performing, when he passed through a field in which was a savage bull. The bull seeing him began to bellow, and run at him with lowered horns. "Now then," said old David, "that note must be double B." He whipped the bass viol out of the green bag, set it down, and drew his bow over the strings, to try to hit the note bellowed. The bull, staggered at the response, stopped, threw up his head, and—turned tail.

But there were musicians of a less dignified character, jolly, reckless, drinking dogs, who fiddled at every festive gathering till they could fiddle no more. They were invariably present at a wedding.

In a popular song called Chummie's Wedding, it is said of the merry-makers—

"The fiddler did stop, and he struck up a hop,
Whilst seated on top of a trunk,
But not one of the batch could come up to the scratch,
They were all so outrageously drunk."

Very quaint old tunes were played; as the space for dancing in cottages was extremely limited, the performance was often confined to one couple, sometimes to a single performer—a man, who took off his shoes and went through really marvellous steps. The step-dance is now gone, or all but gone, but was at one time much cultivated among the peasantry of the west of England. Much depended on the fiddler, who played fast or slow, and changed his air, the dancer altering his pace and step, and the whole character of his dance, to suit the music.

The village clerk was generally the great musical authority in the parish; he led the orchestra in the church, and not unusually also played at merry-makings. It may be remembered that in Doctor Syntax is a plate representing the parson in his black cocked hat and bushy wig performing on his violin to the rustics as they dance about the May-pole; and again, fiddling, he leads the harvest-home procession. Such conduct would be regarded as highly indecorous now; but was there harm in it? Was it not well that the parson should be associated with the merry-makings of his flock? that he should lead and direct their music?

Those old orchestras were, I fear, subject to outbreaks of discord, and that was one reason why they were displaced first by the barrel organ, then by the harmonium. Well, but the solar envelope is always torn by tempests, and yet it diffuses a light in which we live and enjoy ourselves, regardless of these storms. The very necessity for living together in some sort of agreement, in order that they might be able to perform concerted pieces, was of educative advantage to the old musicians. It taught them to subdue their individuality to the common welfare. And so, not only because it gave more persons an interest in the conduct of Divine worship than at present is the case, but also because the orchestra was a great educative school of self-control, its disappearance from every village is to be regretted.

CHAPTER XI

THE VILLAGE BARD

IN the Vicar of Wakefield, the parsonage is visited periodically by a poor man of the name of Burchell. "He was fondest of the company of children, whom he used to call harmless little men. He was famous, I found, for singing them ballads and telling them stories.... He generally came for a few days into our neighbourhood once a year, and lived upon the neighbours' hospitality. He sat down to supper among us, and my wife was not sparing of her gooseberry wine. The tale went round; he sung us old songs, and gave the children the story of the Buck of Beverland, with the history of Patient Grizzel, the Adventures of Catskin, and then Fair Rosamund's Bower."

How completely the itinerant singer of ballads and teller of folk-tales has disappeared—driven from the houses of the gentle, because the young people have books now, and amuse themselves with them, and he lingers on only in the ale-houses; such men are few and far between, feeble old men, who can now hardly obtain a hearing for their quaint stories, and whose minor melodies are voted intolerable by young ears, disciplined only to appreciate music-hall inanities.

There are still a few of these men about, and as I have taken a good deal of pains to get into their confidence, and collect from them the remains—there exist only remains—of their stories, musical and poetical, I am able to give an account of them which ought to interest, for the old village bard or song-man is rapidly becoming as extinct as the dodo and the great auk.

The village bard or song-man is the descendant of the minstrel. Now the minstrels were put down by Act of Parliament in 1597, and were to be dealt with by the magistrates with severity as rogues and vagabonds. That sealed the doom of the old ballad. All such as were produced later are tame and flat in comparison with the genuine songs of the old times, and can at best be regarded only as modern imitations. The press has preserved in Broadsides a good number of ballads, and The Complete Dancing Master and other collections have saved a good number of the old tunes from being irrevocably lost. But by no means all were thus preserved; a great many more continued to be sung by our peasantry, and I quite believe the old men when they say, that at one time they knew some one hundred and fifty to two hundred distinct songs and melodies; their memories were really extraordinary. But then they could neither read nor write, and the faculty of remembering was developed in them to a remarkable extent. I have heard of two of these men meeting to sing against each other for a wager. They began at sunset; one started a ballad, sang it through, then his opponent sang one, and so on. The object was to ascertain which knew most. The sun rose on them, and neither had come to an end of his store, so the stakes were drawn.

These old minstrels all are in the same tale, when asked to sing, "Lord, your honour, I haven't a sung these thirty year. Volks now don't care to hear my songs. Most on 'em be gone right out o' my head." Yet a good many come back; and I find that when I read over the first verse or two of a series of ballads in any collection, that the majority are either known to them, or suggest to them another, or a variant.

It is not ballads only that are stored in their memories—many ballads that go back for their origin to before the reign of Henry VII., but also songs that breathe the atmosphere of the time of Elizabeth. Mr. R. Bell, in his introduction to his Songs from the Dramatists, says, "The superiority in all qualities of sweetness, thoughtfulness, and purity of the writers of the sixteenth century over their successors is strikingly exhibited in these productions.

"The songs of the age of Elizabeth and James I. are distinguished as much by their delicacy and chastity of feeling, as by their vigour and beauty. The change that took place under Charles II. was sudden and complete. With the Restoration love disappears, and sensuousness takes its place. Voluptuous without taste or sentiment, the songs of that period may be said to dissect in broad daylight the life of the town, laying bare with revolting shamelessness the tissues of its most secret vices. But as this morbid anatomy required some variation to relieve its sameness, the song sometimes transported the libertinism into the country, and through the medium of a sort of Covent Garden pastoral exhibited the fashionable delinquencies in a masquerade of Strephons and Chlorises, no better than the Courtalls and Loveits of the comedies. The costume of innocence gave increased zest to the dissolute wit, and the audiences seem to have been delighted with the representation of their own licentiousness in the transparent disguise of verdant images, and the affectation of rural simplicity."

Very few of the songs of the Restoration have lingered on in the memory of our minstrels, if ever they were taken into their store. Many of the songs of that period were set to tunes that have passed on from generation to generation, up to the present age, when they are all being neglected for wretched, vulgar songs, without fun and without melody. The ballad especially is death-smitten. Folks nowadays lack patience, and will not endure a song that is not finished in three minutes. The old ballad was a folk-tale run into jingling rhyme, and sung to a traditional air; it is often very long. One I have recovered, The Gipsy Countess, runs through over twenty verses. The very popular Saddle to Rags runs through some twenty-two, Lord Bateman has about fifty, and Arthur of Bradley has hardly any end to it. A ballad cannot be pared down greatly, as that destroys the story, which is set to verse to be told leisurely, with great variety of expression.

In 1846 the Percy Society issued to its members a volume entitled Ancient Poems, Ballads, and Songs of the Peasantry of England, edited by Mr. J. H. Dixon, who gives in his preface the following account of the sources whence he collected them:—"He who, in travelling through the rural districts of England, has made the roadside inn his resting-place, who has visited the lowly dwellings of the villagers and yeomanry, and been present at their feasts and festivals, must have observed that there are certain old poems, ballads, and songs which are favourites with the masses, and have been said and sung from generation to generation." When I was a boy I was wont to ride about my native county, putting up at little village inns for the night, and there I often came in for gatherings where the local song-man entertained the company. Unfortunately I did not make any collection at the time, though snatches of the songs and wafts of the strains lingered in my head. I dare say that there are still singers of ballads in other parts of England, but my researches have been confined to the west. Somerset had its own type of songs with peculiar cadences, and Devon and Cornwall were rich to overflow in melodies. Wherever I go in quest of a song-man, I hear the same story, "Ah! there was old So-and-so, eighty years of age, died last winter of bronchitis, he was a singer and no mistake." They have been struck down, those old men, and therefore we must prize the more those that are left.

Anciently—well, not so very anciently either, for it was within my memory—almost every parish had its bard, a man generally the descendant of a still more famous father, who was himself but the legatee of a race of song-men. This village bard had his memory stored with traditional melodies and songs and ballads, committed to him as a valuable deposit by his father, wedded to well-known ancient airs, and the country singer not only turned from the affectation of the new melodies, but with jealous tenacity clung to

111

the familiar words. Words became so wedded to airs that the minstrels, and their hearers and imitators, could not endure to have them dissociated.

I had an instance of this three winters ago, when, at a village concert, I sang an old ballad, The Sun was Set behind the Hill, set by a friend to a melody he had composed for it.

A very old labourer who was present began to grumble. "He's gotten the words right, but he's not got the right tune. He should zing 'un right or not at all," and he got up and left the room in disdain.

The village minstrel did certainly compose some of the melodies he sang, generally to a new ballad, or song that was acquired from a broadside, or to one he had himself made. This the old men have distinctly assured me of. They did not all, or a large number of them did not, pretend to the faculty of musical composition, but they have named to me men so gifted, and have told me of melodies they composed. There was, and is, a blacksmith in a remote village in Devon, who is reported to be able to play any musical instrument put into his hands, at all events after a little trial of its peculiarities. He is said to be able to set any copy of verses offered him to original melodies.

Davey, the writer of Will Watch, and other pleasant songs of the Dibdin period and character, was a Devonshire blacksmith. But, as already hinted, these men also composed verses. There was such an one, a village poet in the parish where I lived as a child. His story was curious. He had bought his wife in Okehampton market for half-a-crown. Her husband, weary of her temper and tongue, brought her to the "Gigglet" fair with a rope round her neck, and the minstrel had the hardihood to buy her. I know that it has often been charged by foreigners on English people that they sell their wives thus, but this was a fact. The woman was so sold, and so bought; the buyer and seller quite believed that the transaction was legal. She lived with the purchaser till her death, and a very clean, decent, hard-working woman she was. She had, indeed, a tongue; but when she began to let it wag, then the minstrel clapped his hands to his ears, ran out of the house, and betook himself to the ale-house, where he was always welcome, and from which he did not himself return, but was conveyed home—in a wheel-barrow. This man regarded himself as the poet of the place, and nothing of importance took place in my grandfather's family without his coming to the house to sing a copy of verses he had composed on the occasion. Many a good laugh was had over his verses, which, like those of Orlando, "had in them more feet than the verses would bear; and the feet were lame, and could not bear themselves without the verse."

There was one, made on the occasion of some new arrangement with the farmers relative to the game entered into by my father, and which gave general satisfaction, of which each stanza ended with the refrain—

> "For he had, he had, he had, he had,
> O he had a most expansive mind."

The reader will conclude that the world has not lost much in that Jim's poems have not been preserved.

One very odd feature, by the way, of these singers is the manner in which they manufacture syllables where the verse halts. Thus when "gold-en" comes in place of two trochees, they convert it into "guddle-old-en"; even, when the line is still more halting, into "gud-dle-udd-le-old-en." In like manner "soul" or "tree" is turned into "suddle-ole" or "tur-rur-ree."

There was another village poet who flourished in the same epoch as the Jim cited above. His name was Rab Downe. He had a remarkable facility for running off impromptu verses. On one occasion at a wrestling match, he began swinging himself from foot to foot, and to a chant—these fellows always sing their verses— described the match as it went on before him, versifying all the turns and incidents of the struggle, throwing in words relative to the onlookers, their names and complementary expletives.

No doubt that much of the compositions of these men was mere doggerel, but it was not always so. In their songs gleam out here and there a poetic, or, at all events, a fresh and quaint thought. What is always difficult to ascertain is what is original and what traditional, for when they do pretend to originality they often import into their verses whole passages from ancient ballads. But in this they are not peculiar. Hindley in his Life of James Catnach, the Broadside publisher, gives some verses on the death of the Princess Charlotte, which Catnach claimed as his own composition. The first verse runs—

> "She is gone! sweet Charlotte's gone,
> Gone to the silent bourne;
> She is gone, she's gone for ever more,—
> She never can return."

But this was a mere adaptation of a song of The Drowned Lover, which is a favourite with the old singers—

113

"He is gone! my love is drowned!
My love whom I deplore.
He is gone! he's gone! I never,
No I never shall see him more."

Catnach corruscated into brilliant originality in the next
stanza—

"She is gone with her joy—her darling boy,
The son of Leopold, blythe and keen;
She Died the sixth of November,
Eighteen hundred and seventeen."

There is nothing like this in the original Drowned Lover that
influenced the opening of his elegy. "Catnach," says Mr. Hindley—
the italics are his own—"made the following lines out of his own
head!" Our village bards never reached a lower bathos. The reader
may perhaps like to hear the story of the lives of some of these old
fellows.

One, James Parsons, a very infirm man, over seventy,
asthmatic and failing, has been a labourer all his life, and for the
greater part of it on one farm. His father was famed through the
whole country side as "The Singing Machine," he was considered to
be inexhaustible. Alas! he is no more, and his old son shakes his
head and professes to have but half the ability, memory, and
musical faculty that were possessed by his father. He can neither
read nor write. From him I have obtained some of the earliest
melodies and most archaic forms of ballads. Indeed the majority of
his airs are in the old church modes, and generally end on the
dominant. At one time his master sent him to Lydford on the edge
of Dartmoor, to look after a farm he had bought. Whilst there,
Parsons went every pay-day to a little moorland tavern, where the
miners met to drink, and there he invariably got his "entertainment"
for his singing. "I'd been zinging there," said he, "one evening till I
got a bit fresh, and I thought 'twere time for me to be off. So I stood
up to go, and then one chap, he said to me, 'Got to the end o' your
zongs, old man?' 'Not I,' said I, 'not by a long ways; but I reckon it
be time for me to be going.' 'Looky here, Jim,' said he. 'I'll give you a
quart of ale for every fresh song you sing us to-night.' Well, your
honour, I sat down again, and I zinged on—I zinged sixteen fresh
songs, and that chap had to pay for sixteen quarts."

"Pints, surely," I said.

"No, zur!" bridling up. "No, zur—not pints, good English

quarts. And then—I hadn't come to the end o' my zongs, only I were that fuddled, I couldn't remember no more."

"Sixteen quarts between feeling fresh and getting fuddled!"

"Sixteen. Ask Voysey; he paid for'n."

Now this Voysey is a man working for me, so I did ask him. He laughed and said, "Sure enough, I had to pay for sixteen quarts that evening."

Another of my old singers is James Olver, a fine, hale old man, with a face fresh as a rose, and silver hair, a grand old patriarchal man, who has been all his life a tanner. He is a Cornishman, a native of St. Kewe. His father was musical, but a Methodist, and so strict that he would never allow his children to sing a ballad or any profane song in his hearing, and fondly fancied that they grew up in ignorance of such things. But the very fact that they were tabooed gave young Olver and his sister a great thirst to learn, digest, and sing them. He acquired them from itinerant ballad-singers, from miners, and from the village song-men.

Olver was apprenticed to a tanner at Liskeard. "Tell'y," said he, "at Liskeard, sixty years ago, all the youngsters on summer evenings used to meet in a field outside the town called Gurt Lane, and the ground were strewed wi' tan, and there every evening us had wrastling (wrestling), and single-stick, and boxing. Look'y here,"—he put his white head near me and raised the hair,—"do'y see now how my head be a cut about? and look to my forehead and cheek as was cut open wi' single-stick. I wor a famous player in them days; and the gentlefolks and ladies 'ud come out and see us at our sports, just as they goes now to cricket-matches."

Whilst the games went on, or between the intervals, songs were sung. "I'll sing'y one," said Olver, "was a favourite, and were sung to encourage the youngsters."

> 1. "I sing of champions bold,
> That wrestled—not for gold;
> And all the cry
> Was 'Will Trefry,'
> That he would win the day.
> So Will Trefry, huzzah!
> The ladies clap their hands and cry,
> 'Trefry! Trefry! huzzah!'
>
> 2. Then up sprang little Jan,
> A lad scarce grown a man.
> He said, 'Trefry,

115

I wot I'll try
A hitch with you this day.'
So little Jan, huzzah!
The ladies clap their hands and cry,
'O little Jan, huzzah!'

3. He stript him to the waist,
He boldly Trefry faced;
'I'll let him know
That I can throw
As well as he to-day.'
So little Jan, huzzah!
And some said so; but others,'No,
Trefry! Trefry! huzzah!'

4. They wrestled on the ground,
His match Trefry had found;
And back he bore
In struggle sore,
And felt his force give way.
So little Jan, huzzah!
So some did say; but others, 'Nay,
Trefry! Trefry! huzzah!'
5. Then with a desperate toss,
Will showed the flying hoss,[8]
And little Jan
Fell on the tan,
And never more he spake.
O! little Jan, alack!
The ladies say, 'Oh, woe's the day!
O! little Jan, alack!'

6. Now little Jan, I ween,
That day had married been;
Had he not died,
A gentle bride
That day he home had led.
The ladies sigh—the ladies cry,
'O! little Jan is dead.'"

---

[8] The Flying Horse is a peculiarly dangerous throw over the head, and usually breaks or severely injures the spine of the wrestler thus thrown.

At Halwell, in North Devon, lives a fine old man named Roger Luxton, aged seventy-six, a great-grandfather, with bright eyes and an intelligent face. He stays about among his grandchildren, but is usually found at the picturesque farm-house of a daughter at Halwell, called Croft. This old man was once very famous as a song-man, but his memory fails him as to a good number of the ballads he was wont to sing. "Ah, your honour," said he, "in old times us used to be welcome in every farm-house, at all shearing and haysel and harvest feasts; but, bless'y! now the farmers' da'ters all learn the pianny, and zing nort but twittery sort of pieces that have nother music nor sense in them; and they don't care to hear us, and any decent sort of music. And there be now no more shearing and haysel and harvest feasts. All them things be given up. 'Tain't the same world as used to be—'taint so cheerful. Folks don't zing over their work, and laugh after it. There be no dances for the youngsters as there used to was. The farmers be too grand to care to talk to us old chaps, and for certain don't care to hear us zing. Why for nigh on forty years us old zinging-fellows have been drove to the public-houses to zing, and to a different quality of hearers too. And now I reckon the labouring folk be so tree-mendious edicated that they don't care to hear our old songs nother. 'Tis all Pop goes the Weasel and Ehren on the Rhine now. I reckon folks now have got different ears from what they used to have, and different hearts too. More's the pity."

In the very heart of Dartmoor lives a very aged blind man, by name Jonas Coaker, himself a poet, after an illiterate fashion. He is only able to leave his bed for a few hours in the day. He has a retentive memory, and recalls many very old ballads. From being blind he is thrown in on himself, and works on his memory till he digs out some of the old treasures buried there long ago. Unhappily his voice is completely gone, so that melodies cannot be recovered through him.

There is a Cornishman whose name I will give as Elias Keate— a pseudonym—a thatcher, a very fine, big-built, florid man, with big, sturdy sons. This man goes round to all sheep-shearings, harvest homes, fairs, etc., and sings. He has a round, rich voice, a splendid pair of bellows; but he has an infirmity, he is liable to become the worse for the liquor he freely imbibes, and to be quarrelsome over his cups. He belongs to a family of hereditary singers and drinkers. In his possession is a pewter spirit-bottle—a pint bottle—that belonged to his great-grandfather in the latter part of the last century. That old fellow used to drink his pint of raw spirit every day; so did the grandfather of Elias; so did the father of Elias; so would Elias—if he had it; but so do not his sons, for they are teetotalers.

Another minstrel is a little blacksmith; he is a younger man than the others, but he is, to me, a valuable man. He was one of fourteen children, and so his mother sent him, when he was four years old, to his grandmother, and he remained with his grandmother till he was ten. From his grandmother he acquired a considerable number of old dames' songs and ballads. His father was a singer; he had inherited both the hereditary faculty and the stock-in-trade. Thus my little blacksmith learned a whole series which were different from those acquired from the grandmother. At the age of sixteen he left home, finding he was a burden, and since that age has shifted for himself. This man tells me that he can generally pick up a melody and retain it, if he has heard it sung once; that of a song twice sung, he knows words and music, and rarely, if ever, requires to have it sung a third time to perfect him.

On the south of Dartmoor live two men also remarkable in their way—Richard Hard and John Helmore. The latter is an old miller, with a fine intelligent face and a retentive memory. He can read, and his songs have to be accepted with caution. Some are very old, others have been picked up from song-books. Hard is a poor cripple, walking only with the aid of two sticks, with sharply-chiselled features,—he must have been a handsome man in his youth,—bright eyes, a gentle, courteous manner, and a marvellous store of old words and tunes in his head. He is now past stone-breaking on the roadside, and lives on £4 per annum. He has a charming old wife; and he and the old woman sing together in parts their quaint ancient ballads. That man has yielded up something like eighty distinct melodies. His memory, however, is failing; for when the first lines of a ballad in some published collection is read to him, he will sometimes say, "I did know that some forty years ago, but I can't sing it through now." However, he can very generally "put the tune to it."

The days of these old singers is over. What festive gatherings there are now are altered in character. The harvest home is no more. We have instead harvest festivals, tea and cake at sixpence a head in the school-room, and a choral service and a sermon in the church. Village weddings are now quiet enough, no feasting, no dancing. There are no more shearing feasts; what remain are shorn of all their festive character. Instead, we have cottage garden produce shows. The old village "revels" linger on in the most emaciated and expiring semblance of the old feast. The old ballad-seller no more appears in the fair. I wrote to a famous broadside house in the west

118

the other day, to ask if they still produced sheet-ballads, and the answer was, "We abandoned that line thirty years ago;" and no one else took it up.

"I love a ballad but even too well," says the Clown in Winter's Tale, and "I love a ballad in print, a'-life!" sighs Mopsa; but there are no Clowns and Mopsas now. Clever Board School scholars and misses who despise ballads, and love dear as life your coarse, vulgar, music-hall buffoonery.

[9]"I reckon the days is departed
When folks 'ud 'a listened to me;
I feels like as one broken-hearted,
A thinking of what used to be.
And I dun' know as much is amended
Than was in them merry old times,
When, wi' pipes and good ale, folks attended
To me and my purty old rhymes.
To me and my purty old rhymes.

'Tes true, I be cruel asthmatic,
I've lost ivry tooth i' my head,
And my limbs be crim'd up wi' rheumatic—
D'rsay I were better in bed.
But Lor'! wi' that dratted blue ribbon,
Tay-totals and chapels—the lot!
A leckturing, canting and fibbin',
The old zinging man is forgot.
The old zinging man is forgot.

I reckon, that wi' my brown fiddle,
I'd go from this cottage to that,
All the youngsters 'ud dance in the middle,
Their pulses and feet pit-a-pat.
I cu'd zing—if you'd stand me the liquor,
All night, and 'ud never give o'er;
My voice—I don't deny't getting thicker,
But never exhausting my store.
But never exhausting my store.

'Tes politics now is the fashion,

_____

[9] From Songs of the West, by S. Baring Gould and H. Fleetwood Sheppard. Methuen & Co.: 1889.

119

As sets folks about by the ear,
And slops makes the poorest o' lushing,
No zinging for me wi'out beer.
I reckon the days be departed
For such jolly gaffers as I;
Folks will never again be light-hearted,
As they was in the days that's gone by.
As they was in the days that's gone by.

O Lor! what wi' their edi'cation,
And me—neither cipher nor write;
But in zinging the best in the nation,
And give the whole parish delight.
I be going, I reckon, full mellow,
To lay in the churchyard my head;
So say—God be wi' you, old fellow!
The last o' the singers is dead.
The last o' the singers is dead."

CHAPTER XII

OLD SERVANTS

WHEN Doomsday Book was drawn up, there was but one female domestic servant in the county of Devon, that covers one million six hundred and fifty-five thousand acres. When I mentioned that fact to a lady of my acquaintance, she heaved a deep-drawn sigh, and said, "I wish I had lived in the times of Doomsday, and had not been the mistress of that one servant-maid."

I believe that, were we lords of creation to have earlet holes communicating with our lady's bowers, as in the middle ages the ladies of creation had openings into their lords' halls, we would hear that much of their conversation turned on the restlessness and misdemeanours of their female servants. I do not mean for a moment to deny or excuse these defects, but to explain the cause of the restlessness complained of. Polly is out of a situation, she can neither boil a potato properly nor cook a mutton-chop. She advertises in the local paper for a situation as cook, from her parents' cottage, where the whole family pig in one room. The post arrives next morning with forty or fifty answers from ladies asking, pleading for her services. Half an hour later up drives a squire's carriage with coach and footman on the box, then the humble pony carriage of the rector, next the jingle of a maiden lady who lives two miles off. All day long carriages of every description are staying at the door, and ladies are visiting, entreating for the services of Polly. Polly spreads the forty or fifty letters she has received on the table.

1. "Is there a kitchen-maid kept?" "No." "Then I won't go to you."

2. "What wages?" "Twenty pounds." "I take nothing under twenty-eight, and all found."

3. "Any men-servants?" "A butler." "Married or single?" "Married—wife lives out." "I can go nowhere where there are not one or two unmarried and agreeable footmen."

4. "You want a character, ma'am? Very sorry—if you doubts my respectability we shan't agree."

5. "How many in family?" "Thirteen." "No good. I go nowhere but to a single gentleman who waits on himself, and cooks his own dinner."

6. "Church or chapel, ma'am, did you ask? I keeps my

religious opinions to myself, and won't be dictated to. No female Jesuits for me."

7. "Early riser? No, ma'am, I am not an early riser, and don't intend to demean myself by being such. I expecks a cup o' tea and a slice of bread and butter brought me in bed by the kitchen-maid afore I gets up."

8. "Do I know how to cook entrées? There's nothink I can't do; I can do better than a thousand perfessionals."

9. "Don't allow but alternate Sunday evenings out? I expecks to have wot evenings out I likes."

10. "Object to waste, do you, ma'am. Very sorry, you must go elsewhere. I wastes on principle. I wouldn't be so unladylike as to save what belongs to others. Chuck away what I can't use is my scripture, praises be."

Now is it to be wondered at that with such a crowd of applicants Polly's head should be turned, and that she should think herself the greatest person in the world, so that she will not stay in any place where she has not everything her own way?

Anciently but few people kept servants, and the servants they kept were to a large extent drawn from their own class, were often their own relatives. Pepys took his own sister to be servant in his house. 1660, Nov. 12. "My father and I discoursed seriously about my sister coming to live with me, and yet I am much afraid of her ill-nature. I told her plainly my mind was to have her come, not as a sister but as a servant, which she promised me she could, and with many thanks did weep for joy." 1660-1, Jan. 2. "Home to dinner, where I found Pal (my sister) was come; but I do not let her sit down at the table with me, which I do at first that she may not expect it hereafter from me."

Sister Paulina's temper proved unendurable. On November 12, 1662, Pepys writes—"By my wife's appointment came two young ladies, sisters, acquaintances of my wife's brothers, who are desirous to wait upon some ladies, and who proffer their services to my wife. The youngest hath a good voice, and sings very well, besides other good qualitys, but I fear hath been bred up with too great libertys for my family, and I fear greater inconveniences of expenses—though I confess the gentlewoman being pretty handsome and singing, makes me have a good mind to her." This girl, the younger Gosnell, was engaged. On the 22nd he writes, "This day I bought the book of country dances against my wife's woman Gosnell comes, who dances finely."

On November 29. "My wife and I in discourse do pleasantly call Gosnell over Marmotte."

On January 4, 1662-3. "My wife did propound my having of my sister Pal again to be her woman, since one we must have."— Gosnell had been required to attend on her uncle, a justice.—"It being a great trouble to me that I should have a sister of so ill a nature, that I must be forced to spend money upon a stranger, when it might better be upon her if she were good for anything."

Here are a couple of entries that came close together in the register of Ottery St. Mary concerning marriages—

"1657, September 7. George Trobridge, Gentleman, servant unto John Vaughan, Esq., married Elizabeth, daughter of Nicolas Hancock."

"1658, April 8. Jonathan Browne, of Bridport, Gent, and Margaret Harris, servant to Richard Arundell, gent."

That Margaret Harris was a gentlewoman admits of little doubt. In the register of Woolbrough I remember seeing that the Yarde family of Bradley had a cousin or two of the same name in service in their house.

The usual term for a valet to a man of estate was—his gentleman, and a lady's maid-servant was—her gentlewoman. The apostle commands, "By love serve one another," and our forefathers do not seem at one time to have thought that domestic service was derogatory to gentility; and I do not myself see how that any one who considers that his supreme Master and Lord humbled Himself, and took upon Him the form of a servant, and stooped to wash His disciples feet, can sneer at menial service. Nothing is menial but what is done in a base, cantankerous, unloving spirit. It is usually found that such domestics as come out of the lowest slums are they who are most particular not to do anything that is not precisely their work, who are most choice and most exacting. When the relatives of the family ceased to be servants in the house, then came in the daughters of farmers, the cleanest, most thrifty, obliging, sensible, and altogether admirable domestics that ever were. Who that is over fifty does not remember them? They were conscientious, they took an interest in the family, their mistresses liked—even loved them.

Then the farmers became too grand in their ideas to send out their girls into service, and consequently one class alone was drained of its young women, the labourer class, the uneducated, undisciplined, the class that had no idea of thrift; and is it to be wondered at that the girls' heads should be turned when they find in what demand they were? I do not mean to say that, taken as a whole, a more respectable, nice, honest, cleanly set of girls is anywhere to be found than our English serving lasses; but we live in an age of transition—they who were formerly only required as drudges in farm-houses, suddenly discover themselves in huge request, and that has upset them.

The trouble there is in households now about domestic servants is said by some to be due to the mistresses—they do not make friends of their slavies, as did the ancient mistresses of theirs. But how can they, when the girl does not stay in the house over three months or half a year, and when she belongs to a class intellectually, socially, educationally removed from her mistress by a great cultural gulf as wide as that which separated Lazarus from Dives?

There are few more charming figures in fiction and in retrospect than the "old blue-coated serving-man," devoted to his master's interests, and living and dying in his service; but I doubt whether he deserved the halo with which he has been invested. He was a bit of an imposture. Devoted he was to his master's interests, because he lived on his master, and just on the same principle as any parasite desires the welfare, the fatness, and full-bloodedness of the mammal on which it is itself battening. A French cynic in his will bequeathed to his valet "all that of which he has robbed me." There have been old and faithful servants, but that there were many of them unselfseeking I do not believe; and I remember a very considerable number of them who became intolerable nuisances— exacting, despotic, believing that the family on which they depended could not get on without them, as the fly said of itself when it sat on the coach, "How I am getting the carriage along!" I also know that a good many have carried on gross depredations on their masters for many years unsuspected and undetected, all the while believed to have but one object of love and care in the world—the master and his house.

If we were to make a graduated scale of servants, according to their merits and demerits, I should put the butler at one end and the coachman at the other; in the former the imposition reaches its maximum, and the minimum is in the coachman, or, to put it the other way, I think that the dear old coachman is the most genuine, true-hearted, and deepest imbued with love of his master and the family, and that there is the least of this unselfish love in the butler. Very ungrateful and unjust would I be were I not to acknowledge the excellence in the old coachman, for have I not one of my own, now indeed for his age dethroned from his box but not from my service, who carried me in his arms to the hayfield when I was a little fellow, hardly able to toddle, and who now loves above everything to take my youngest into the stables, and perch the little fellow on the back of one of the carriage horses. A worthy old servant, who had been with my grandfather, then my father, then with me, and—who knows? for he is green still—may serve my son.

The old notion was, that a servant was engaged for a year, and that a servant could not leave, nor a master discharge a servant, under a quarter's notice. The servants within a house were recognized by law as menials, from the Latin intra menia, within walls. As late as last century, all single men between twelve years old and sixty, and married ones under thirty years of age, and all single women between twelve and forty, not having any visible livelihood, were compellable by two justices to go into service of some sort. The apprentice, from the French apprendre, to learn, was usually bound for a term of years, by indenture, to serve the master, and be maintained and instructed by him. Landowners and farmers had their apprentices as well as their menials. Orphan children were apprenticed by the parish, and an almost filial relation and affection grew up between master and mistress and their apprentices. This was specially noticeable among farm-servants. I knew an old man who had been apprenticed to my great-great-grandmother, that died at the end of last century, and he always spoke of her with the tenderest respect, and was proud to the last hour of his life that he had been apprenticed to the old madame.

The farm-servants and the inferior servants to the gentry were hired at certain fairs, generally at Martinmas; in the west of England these are called giglet fairs, but they exist in Yorkshire, and indeed in many other parts of England. The word giglet means a girl. The girls and young men were wont to stand in rows in the market-place, to be looked at and selected. They wore ribands according to the sort of service they desired to enter upon. A carter carried in his hat a tuft of white ribands, a cook wore a red riband, and a housemaid a bunch of blue. The giglet fairs continue, and are attended by all the labouring population of the country side, especially by the young of both sexes, but there is very little hiring now done at them.

One of the most perplexing facts to the student of genealogy, in making out the pedigree of an important family from registers of births, deaths, and marriages in a parish, is that wherever a great family was seated, there are found also a shoal of individuals, distinctly of an inferior social class, bearing the same patronymic. That these were no blood relatives is almost certain, for they are not mentioned in the wills of those belonging to the aristocratic family; and we find no evidence in registers or elsewhere of any family relation. It has often been conjectured, that these individuals and families did really derive from the main aristocratic stem, perhaps not legitimately but left-handedly. But the evidence for this is wanting—it may be forthcoming here and there in individual cases, but there is no proof that this was generally so. To this day we find among the labourers names of historical and great landed families, and we are disposed to think that these are actual lineal offshoots from such families, and sometimes fancy we trace a certain dignity of bearing and aristocratic cast in their features. But I believe that these humble Courtenays, Cliffords, Veres, Devereux, &c., have not a drop of the blood in their veins belonging to these great families, that, in fact, they are descendants of menial servants, who were once in the castle or manor-house of these barons and knights and squires, and that they ate their beef and drank their ale, but drew no blood from their veins. In the fifteenth century surnames were by no means general, and even in the sixteenth were not of general adoption. To this day in the western hills of Yorkshire, separating that county from Lancashire, persons are known by their pedigrees, and very often their surnames are generally unknown. Tom is not Tom Greenwood, but Tom o' Jakes, that is, Tom the son of Jack; and if there be two Toms in a parish both sons of Jack, then one is distinguished from the other by carrying the pedigree further back a stage. One is Tom o' Jakes o' Will's, and the other is Tom o' Jakes o' Harry's. In early parish registers such an entry as this may occur—

"1596, 3 July. Buried, William, servant to Arthur Carew, Esq., commonly called William Carew."

Later than that—in 1660-1—Pepys enters on Feb. 14, "My boy Wareman (his servant lad) hath all this day been called young Pepys, as Sir W. Pen's boy (servant) is young Pen."

At the end of last century and the beginning of this it was a common custom for servant men to assume the titles of their masters, and to address each other under their master's names. This was not an affectation, it was a survival of the old custom of every servant taking his master's surname, as he wore his livery.

In High Life Below Stairs we have this scene—

"The Park

Duke's servant. What wretches are ordinary servants, that go on in the same vulgar track every day! eating, working, and sleeping!—But we, who have the honour to serve the nobility, are of another species. We are above the common forms, have servants to wait upon us, and are as lazy and luxurious as our masters. Ha!—my dear Sir Harry—

126

(Enter Sir Harry's Servant.)

How have you done these thousand years?

Sir H.'s serv. My Lord Duke!—your grace's most obedient servant!

Duke's serv. Well, Baronet, and where have you been?

Sir H.'s serv. At Newmarket, my Lord.—We have had dev'lish fine sport.

After a while they retire, then enter Lady Bab's Maid and Lady Charlotte's Maid.

Lady B.'s maid. O fie, Lady Charlotte! you are quite indelicate. I am sorry for your taste.

Lady C.'s maid. Well, I say it again, I love Vauxhall."

The Spectator (June 11th, 1711) says, "Falling in the other Day at a Victualling-House near the House of Peers, I heard the Maid come down and tell the Landlady at the Bar, That my Lord Bishop swore he would throw her out at Window, if she did not bring up more Mild Beer, and that my Lord Duke would have a double Mug of Purle. My Surprize was encreased, in hearing loud and rustick Voices speak and answer to each other upon the publick Affairs, by the Names of the most Illustrious of our Nobility; till of a sudden one came running in, and cry'd the House was rising. Down came all the Company together, and away! The Alehouse was immediately filled with Clamour, and scoring one Mug to the Marquis of such a Place, Oyl and Vinegar to such an Earl, three Quarts to my new Lord for wetting his Title, and so forth.... It is a common Humour among the Retinue of People of Quality, when they are in their Revels, ... to assume in a humorous Way the Names and Titles of those whose Liveries they wear."

What was done in a "humorous Way" in the days of Addison, was a relic of what was actually done in sober seriousness a couple of centuries earlier, when surnames were possessed by the few only, and these men of consequence.

Does the reader remember the charming account of the servants in the household of Sir Roger de Coverly? "There is one Particular which I have seldom seen but at Sir Roger's; it is usual in all other Places, that Servants fly from the Parts of the House through which their Master is passing; on the contrary, here they industriously place themselves in his way; and it is on both Sides, as it were, understood as a Visit, when the Servants appear without calling.... Thus Respect and Love go together; and a certain

127

Chearfulness in Performance of their Duty is the particular Distinction of the lower Part of his Family. When a Servant is called before his Master, he does not come with an Expectation to hear himself rated for some trivial Fault, threatned to be stripped, or used with any other unbecoming Language, which mean Masters often give to worthy Servants; but it is often to know, what Road he took that he came so readily back according to Order; whether he passed by such a Ground; if the old Man who rents it is in good health: or whether he gave Sir Roger's Love to him, or the like.

"A Man who preserves a Respect, founded on his Benevolence to his Dependants, lives rather like a Prince than a Master in his Family; his Orders are received as Favours, rather than Duties; and the Distinction of approaching him is Part of the Reward for executing what is commanded by him."

It is singular to see how small the wages paid were formerly for domestics, and what a leap up they have made of late, synchronous with deterioration of quality and character. For a farmer's daughter £7 was a high wage, and now £17 is sniffed at by a ploughman's wench. Pepys took a cook from the house of his Grace the Duke of Albemarle, and paid her £4 per annum, and complains at the wage. He says he never before did spend so big a sum on a wage. She must have been an energetic and active woman, for here is the menu of a dinner she cooked. "We had a fricasee of rabbits and chickens, a leg of mutton boiled, three carps in a dish, a great dish of a side of lamb, a dish of roasted pigeons, a dish of four lobsters, three tarts, a lamprey pie, a most rare pie, a dish of anchovies, good wine of several sorts—most neatly dressed by our own only mayde." How did she manage it without a kitchen range with hot plates?

The account-book of Mrs. Joyce Jefferies, a lady resident in Herefordshire and Worcestershire during the Civil War, comprises the receipt and expenditure of nine years. She lived a single person in her house in Hereford, and by no means on a contracted scale. Many female servants are mentioned, two having wages from £3 to £3 4s. per annum, with gowns of dark stuff at midsummer. Her coachman, receiving 40s. per annum, had at Whitsuntide, 1639, a new cloth suit and cloak; and when he was dressed in his best, wore fine blue silk ribbon at the knees of his hose. The liveries of this and another man-servant were, in 1641, of green Spanish cloth, and cost upwards of nine pounds. Her steward received a salary of £5 16s., and she kept for him a horse, which he rode to collect her rents and dues, and to see to the management of her estate.

I have myself a book of accounts, a little later, where the "mayde of my wyfe" gets £3, and the footman £4 and his livery.

In some houses a whole series of account-books has been preserved, showing, among other things, the rise in wages paid for servants, and very instructive they are.

Here is from an account-book of 1777, in a country squire's house. Wages were paid on Lady Day for the whole year, and not quarterly.

1777.	£	s.	d.
Sarah's wages	4	19	0
Old Becky's	3	0	0
Anne, half-year	1	0	0
Nanny	5	5	0
Cook	7	7	0
Gardener	2	7	0
Bray the waggoner	9	0	0
A certain Betty had for wages and bill	6	0	0

In an account-book for 1811 the wages are a little higher—

	£	s.	d.
Footman	10	0	0
Coachman	14	0	0
Cook	8	8	0
Housemaid	6	6	0
Scullery-maid	2	5	0
The Boy	3	0	0

There died only a year ago an old woman who had been a servant since she was eighteen in two of the greatest houses in the neighbourhood. When she first went into service, she told me, it was at K—. She received £4 as her wage, and managed to save money on that. She was, however, given a washing-dress by her mistress at Lady Day. After some years she went to L— Park, where she received £6. This was after a while raised to £7, and she invariably put away some of her wage. When after tried service her wage was raised to £10, the climax of her ambition was reached, she regarded herself as passing rich, and never hoped to obtain more.

"For certain, sir," she said, "my work wasn't worth more."

In my own parish churchyard, one of the best of the monuments is that raised by my grandfather to the memory of an old servant of his grandmother's.

MR. THOMAS HILSDEN,
WHO DIED FEB. 21, 1806,
AGED 70,
HAVING LIVED IN THE FAMILY OF

MRS. MARGARET GOULD, OF LEW HOUSE,

44 YEARS.
THIS STONE WAS ERECTED
IN CONSIDERATION OF HIS FAITHFUL SERVICE.

There is an ancient family I know of historic dignity. It has lost its ancestral estates, lost almost all of its family portraits; but one great picture remains to it, so poorly painted, that at the sale of the Manor-house and its contents no one would buy it,—it is the portrait of an old servant, a giant, a tall and powerful ranger, who, partly for his size, chiefly for his fidelity, was painted and hung up in the hall along with the knights and squires and ladies of the family which he had served so well.

The mention of this picture leads me to say a few words about a worthy man who died some twenty years ago. Rawle was hind to the late Sir Thomas Acland of Killerton. Sir Thomas introduced Arab blood among the Exmoor ponies, and greatly improved the breed. About 1810 he appointed Rawle in charge of these ponies. He was a fine man, fully six feet high, and big in proportion. His power of breaking in the ponies was extraordinary. He was quite indifferent to falls, often pony and man rolling over and over each other. The sale of the ponies generally took place at Bampton and at Taunton fairs. The system was this—a herd of the wild little creatures was driven into the fair. Buyers attended from all parts of the country, and when a dealer took a fancy to a pony, he pointed him out to the moor-man in attendance, who went into the herd, seized upon the selected one, and brought him out by sheer strength. This is no easy matter, for the Exmoor pony fights with his fore-feet in desperate fashion. It usually took, and takes, two men to do this, but Rawle did not require assistance, such was his strength. Indeed so strong was Rawle, that he would put a hand under the feet of a maid-servant on each side of him, and raise himself and at the same time both of them, till he was upright, and he held each woman on the palm of his hand, one on each side of him, level with his waist. Sir Thomas Acland was wont, when he had friends with him, to get the man to make this exhibition of his strength before them.

Sir Thomas had a hunting box at Higher Combe (called in the district Yarcombe); he occupied one portion of the house when there, a farmer occupied the rest. It was a curious scene—a remnant of feudal times—when Sir Thomas came there. His tenants, summoned for the purpose, had accompanied him in a cavalcade from Winsford, or Hornicott. John Rawle could never be persuaded to eat a bite or take a draught when his master was in a house; he planted himself as a sentry upright before the door when Sir Thomas went in to refresh himself anywhere, and nothing could withdraw him from his post.

In connexion with these expeditions to Higher Combe, it may be added that the cavalcade of tenants would attend Sir Thomas to the wood where a stag had been harboured. Among them was a band, each member of the band played one note only; but it was so arranged that a hunting tune was formed by these notes being played in succession. When the stag was unharboured, and started across the moor, the band commenced this tune, and until it was played out the hounds were kept in leash. The time occupied by this tune was the "law" given to the stag, and when it was ended the hounds were laid on.

A famous china bowl was made in China, and presented to Sir Thomas by the Hunt. This bowl used to be kept at Higher Combe; it represented a stag-hunt. And twelve glasses were presented to Sir Thomas along with it, each engraved with a stag, and the words, "Success to the hunting."

One day Sir Thomas said to Rawle, "Rawle, I want to send a gelding and a mare in foal to Duke Ludwig of Baden, at Baden Baden. Can you take them?"

"Certainly, Sir Thomas."

The man could neither read nor write, and of course knew no other language than the broadest Exmoor dialect—and this was at the beginning of the century, when there were not the facilities for travelling that there are now. He started for Baden Baden, and took his charges there in safety, and delivered them over to the Grand Duke. He had, however, an added difficulty, in that the mare foaled en route, and he had a pass for two ponies only.

Is the old "good and faithful servant" a thing of the past? Not perhaps the good servant, but the servant who continues in a family through the greatest portion of his or her life, who becomes a part of the family, is probably gone for ever; the change in the signification of words tells us of social changes. A man's family, even in Addison's time, comprised his servants. "Of what does your family consist?" A hundred and fifty years ago this would have been answered by an enumeration of those comprising the household, from the children to the scullion. Now who would even think of a servant when such a question is asked? The family is shrunk to the blood-relatives, and the servants are outside the family circle.

We are in a condition of transformation in our relations to our servants; we no longer dream of making them our friends, and consequently they no longer regard us with devotion. But I am not sure that the fault lies with the master. The spirit of unrest is in the land; the uneducated and the partially educated crave for excitement, and find it in change; they can no longer content themselves with remaining in one situation, and when the servants shift quarters every year or two, how can master and mistress feel affection for them, or take interest in them?

Does the reader know Swift's Rules and Directions for Servants? They occupy one hundred and eighteen pages of volume twelve of his works, in the edition of 1768, and comprise instructions to butler, cook, footman, coachman, groom, steward, chambermaid, housemaid, nurse, etc. They show us that human nature among servants was much the same in the middle of last century as in this. Only a scanty extract must be given.

"When your master or lady calls a servant by name, if that servant be not in the way, none of you are to answer, for then there will be no end of your drudgery.

"When you have done a fault be always pert and insolent, and behave yourself as if you were the injured person.

"The cook, the butler, the groom, and every other servant should act as if his master's whole estate ought to be applied to that particular servant's business.

"Take all tradesmen's parts against your master. You are to consider if your master hath paid too much, he can better afford the loss than a poor tradesman.

"Never submit to stir a finger in any business but that for which you were particularly hired. For example, if the groom be drunk or absent, and the butler be ordered to shut the stable-door, the answer is ready, 'An' please, your honour, I don't understand horses.'

"If you find yourself to grow into favour with your master or lady, take some opportunity to give them warning, and when they ask the reason, and seem loath to part with you, answer that a poor servant is not to be blamed if he strives to better himself. Upon which, if your master hath any generosity, he will add five or ten shillings a quarter rather than let you go.

"Write your own name and your sweetheart's with the smoke of a candle on the roof of the kitchen, to show your learning. If you are a young sightly fellow, whenever you whisper your mistress at the table, run your nose full into her cheek, or breathe full in her face.

"Never come till you have been called three or four times, for none but dogs will come at the first whistle.

"When you have broken all your earthen vessels below stairs—which is usually done in a week—the copper-pot will do as well; it can boil milk, heat porridge, hold small beer—apply it indifferently to all these uses, but never wash or scour it.

"Although you are allowed knives for the servants' hall at meals, yet you ought to spare them, and make use of your master's.

"Let it be a constant rule, that no chair or table in the servants' hall have above three legs.

"Quarrel with each other as much as you please, only always bear in mind that you have a common enemy, which is your master and lady.

"When your master and lady go abroad together to dine, you need leave only one servant in the house to answer the door and attend the children. Who is to stay at home is to be determined by short and long cuts, and the stayer at home may be comforted by a visit from a sweetheart.

"When your master or lady comes home, and wants a servant who happens to be abroad, your answer must be, that he had but just that minute stepped out, being sent for by a cousin who was dying. When you are chidden for a fault, as you go out of the room mutter loud enough to be plainly heard.

"When your lady sends for you to her chamber to give you orders, be sure to stand at the door and keep it open, fiddling with the lock all the while she is talking to you.

"When you want proper instruments for any work you are about, use all expedients you can invent. For instance, if the poker be out of the way, stir the fire with the tongs; if the tongs be not at hand, use the muzzle of the bellows, the wrong end of the shovel, or the handle of the fire-brush. If you want paper to singe a fowl, tear the first book you see about the house. Wipe your shoes, for want of a clout, on the bottom of a curtain or a damask napkin.

133

"There are several ways of putting out a candle, and you ought to be instructed in them all: you may run the candle-end against the wainscot, which puts the snuff out immediately; you may lay it on the ground and tread the snuff out with your foot; you may hold it upside down until it is choked in its own grease, or cram it into the socket of the candlestick; you may whirl it round in your hand till it goes out.

"Clean your plate, wipe your knives, and rub the dirty tables with the napkins and tablecloths used that day, for it is but one washing.

"When a butler cleans the plate, leave the whiting plainly to be seen in all the chinks, for fear your lady should not believe you had cleaned it.

"You need not wipe your knife to cut bread for the table, because in cutting a slice or two it will wipe itself.

"A butler must always put his finger into every bottle to feel whether it be full.

"Whet the backs of your knives until they are as sharp as the edge, that when gentlemen find them blunt on one side they may try the other.

"Cooks should scrape the bottom of pots and kettles with a silver spoon, for fear of giving them a taste of copper.

"Get three or four charwomen to attend you constantly in the kitchen, whom you pay with the broken meat, a few coals, and all the cinders.

"Never make use of a spoon in anything that you can do with your hands, for fear of wearing out your master's plate.

"In roasting and boiling use none but the large coals, and save the small ones for the fires above stairs." And so on.

If the old servants had their merits, they had also their demerits. Have they not bequeathed the latter to their successors, and carried away their merits with them into a better world?

CHAPTER XIII

THE HUNT

THE genuine Englishman loves a hunt, loves sport, above everything else; I do not mean only those who can afford to ride and shoot, but every Englishman born and bred in the country.

One day the masons were engaged on my house, on the top of a scaffold, the carpenters were occupied within laying a floor, some painters were employed on doors and windows, the gardener was putting into a bed some roses; in the back-yard a youth was chopping up wood; in the stable-yard the coachman was washing the body of the carriage, and in the stable itself the groom was currycombing a horse. Suddenly from the hillside opposite, mantled with oak, came the sound of the hounds in cry, and then the call of the horn. Down from the scaffold came the masons, head over heels, at the risk of their necks; out through the windows shot the carpenters and painters, throwing aside hammers, nails, paint-pot and brushes; down went the roses in the garden; from behind the house leaped the wood-chopper; the coach was left half-washed, and the horse half-currycombed; and over the lawn and through the grounds, regardless of everything, went a wild excited throng of masons, carpenters, woodcutter, coachman, stable-boy, gardener, my own sons, then my own self, having dropped pen, and, forgotten on the terrace was left only the baby—a male, erect in its perambulator, with arms extended, screaming to follow the rout and go after the hounds. Let agitators come and storm and denounce in the midst of our people; they cannot rouse them to fury against the gentry, because they and the gentry run after the hounds together, enjoy a hunt together, and are the best of friends in the field. No, the great socialistic revolution will not take place till the hunt is abolished. That is the great solvent of all prejudices, that the great festival that binds all in one common bond of sympathy.

This season there has appeared at our meets an old man of seventy-five, who was for many years a butler to a rector, a quiet, studious man, who died a few years ago. After the death of his master the butler retired on his savings, and built himself a house. Then—this winter he appeared on a cob at the meet of the foxhounds. "Sir," said he to the Master, "now the ambition of my life is satisfied. Since I was a boy I have wished, and all my days have worked, that I might have a cob on which I could hunt."

Alas! the old fellow found himself so stiff after the first hunt, that at the next meet of the harriers he appeared on foot. He had walked four miles to it; and he ran with the hounds, and was in at the death. After the hunt he walked home hot and happy, and elastic in step.

The farmers naturally like a hunt, as it affords them, apart from the sport, an occasion of showing off and selling their horses. The workmen like a hunt, especially after the hare, for it forms a break in their work. They have their half day's sport, and their masters pay wage just the same as if they had been at work.

The hare hunt naturally lends itself to footers, as the hare runs in a circle, and not straight with the wind in his tail like reynard. Here and there is to be found a cantankerous farmer who objects to having his hedges broken down and his land trampled by the hunters, but he is looked on with distrust and dislike by all in every class, and spoken of as a curmudgeon. Of course, also, there are to be found men who trap and kill foxes, but I verily believe those men's consciences sting them far more on this account than if they had committed a fraud or become drunk. And—by the way, that reminds me of a story.

There came a Hungarian nobleman, whom we will call the Baron Hounymhum, to England. His Christian name was Arpad. He came to England, having a title, but having nothing else; he came, in fact, to seek there his fortune. Belonging to a good family, he was well supplied with letters of introduction, and he was received into society. On more than one occasion he donned his uniform, and had reason to believe that the uniform as well as his handsome face was much admired by the ladies, and envied by the men. Among the acquaintances he made was the Hon. Cecil Blank, through whom he was introduced to one of the first clubs in Piccadilly. He also got acquainted with Lord Ashwater. This nobleman was fond of collecting around him notabilities of all kinds, literary, scientific, and political. He himself was in his politics an advanced Liberal.

The Baron Arpad found, to his astonishment, soon after his arrival in town, that a rumour had got about that he had been implicated in an attempt to assassinate his most gracious sovereign Franz Joseph, King of Hungary and Bohemia, and Emperor of Austria. The idea was absolutely baseless. The fact that he was received at the embassy ought to have shut men's mouths, but no—he was credited with having contrived an infernal machine for the destruction of his beloved sovereign.

He found, to his amazement, that this rumour did him good. He became an interesting foreigner; hitherto he had been only a foreigner. Quite an eager feeling manifested itself among persons of rank and position for having him at their parties; not only so, but he was solicited by magazine editors to write for them articles on the Anarchist party in Hungary and Austria.

Scarce had this odious rumour died away, before he became the victim of another, equally false and equally detestable. A distant cousin, the Baron Adorian Hounymhum, ran away with the Princess Nornenstein, the mother of three sweet little children. The elopement caused a great sensation at Vienna, as the princess was much esteemed by her Majesty the Empress. Prince Nornenstein pursued the fugitives, overtook them in Belgium, fought a duel with the baron, and was shot through the heart.

Well, the report got about that it was Baron Arpad who had run away with the princess, ruined her home, deprived her sweet children of father and mother, and shot the aggrieved husband. It was in vain for him to protest, he was credited with these infamies— and rose in popular estimation. The Duchess of Belgravia at once invited him to her dances. The ladies now courted his society, as before the gentlemen had courted it, when they held him to be a would-be regicide. These two rumours, crediting him with crimes of which he was incapable, did a great deal towards pushing him in society.

Among the many acquaintances the Baron made in town was Mr. Wildbrough, a country squire, M.F.H., a man of wealth, and an M.P. for his county. He had but one daughter, who would be his heiress, and who did not seem insensible to the good looks of the Baron. Now, thought the Hungarian, his opportunity had arrived. The position of landed proprietor in England was in prospect. Moreover, Mr. Wildbrough had invited the Baron to come to Wildbrough Hall in October to see the first meet of the foxhounds.

At the time appointed the Baron arrived, and was cordially received by the squire; Mrs. Wildbrough was gracious, but not gushing; Mary Wildbrough was manifestly pleased to see him—the tell-tale blood assured him of that.

A large party was assembled at the hall for the first meet of the season. The masters of other packs in the county were present. The meet was picturesque, the run excellent. The Baron was in at the death, and received the brush, which he at once presented to Mary Wildbrough. He had ridden beside her, and he felt that his prospects were brightening. He proposed to make the offer that evening at the dance after dinner, when, at Mary's particular request, he was to appear in his Magyar Hussar uniform, in which, as he well knew, he would be irresistible. The Baron took in Mary to dinner, and had an agreeable chat with her, which was only interrupted by Sir Harry Treadwin, a sporting baronet, who said across the table to him, "Baron, I suppose that you have foxes in Hungary?"

"Oh, yes," answered he, "I have shot as many as five or six in a day."

The Baron spoke loud, so as to be heard by all. He was quite unprepared for the consequences. Sir Harry stared at him as at a ghost, with eyes and nostrils and mouth distended. A dead silence fell on the whole company. The host's red face changed colour, and became as collared brawn. The master of another pack became purple as a plum. Mrs. Wildbrough fanned herself vigorously. Mary became white as a lily and trembled, whilst tears welled up in her beautiful eyes. The lady of the house bowed to the lady whom the squire had taken in, and in silence all rose, and the ladies without a word left the room.

The gentlemen remained; conversation slowly unthawed. The Baron turned to the gentleman nearest him, and spoke about matters of general interest. He answered shortly, almost rudely, and turned to converse with his neighbour on the other side. Then the Baron addressed Sir Harry, but he seemed deaf, he stared icily, but made no reply. It was a relief to an intolerable restraint when the gentlemen joined the ladies.

The Baron knew that with his handsome face and gorgeous uniform he could command as many partners in the dance as he desired; but what was his chagrin to find that his anticipations were disappointed. One young lady was engaged, another did not dance the mazurka, a third had forgotten the lancers, a fourth was tired, and a fifth indisposed. After a while he seized his chance, and caught Mary Wildbrough in the conservatory,—she was crying.

"Miss Wildbrough," said he, "are you ill? What ails you?"

"Oh, Baron!" Then she burst into an uncontrollable flood of tears. "I am so—so unhappy! Five or six foxes! Oh, Baron Hounymhum!"

Next day he left. His host would not shake hands with him when he departed. On reaching town he felt dull, and sauntered to the club, but no one would speak to him there. Next day he received this letter from the secretary—

"The secretary of the —— Club regrets to be obliged to inform the Baron Hounymhum that he can no longer be considered the guest of the Club."

After that London society was sealed to him. It was nothing that he had been thought guilty of an attempt to assassinate his sovereign, nothing that he was thought to have eloped with a married woman, wrecked her home and shot her husband, but that he should have shot foxes was The Unpardonable Sin.

We have a peculiar institution in the county of Devon—a week of hare-hunting on Dartmoor after hare-hunting has ceased everywhere else. Dartmoor is a high elevated region totally treeless, with peaks covered with granite, having brawling streams that foam down the valleys between. One main road crosses this vast desolate region, as far as Two Bridges, where is an inn, The Saracen's Head, and there it divides, and runs for many miles more over moor to Moreton Hampstead on one side, and to Ashburton on the other. In the fork of this Y stands an eminently picturesque rugged tor, crested by and strewn with granite, called Bellever. About Easter—anyhow, after hare-hunting has ceased elsewhere—the country-side gathers at Bellever for a week, and nothing can be conceived more changed than the scene at this time from the usual solitude and stillness. The tor is covered with horses, traps, carriages, footers; and if the spring sun be shining, nothing can well be more picturesque.

Whatever may be said or sung to the contrary, hunting on Dartmoor is dangerous work. There are no hedges there, only walls, and these walls are set up round what are locally termed "takes," or enclosures, and are made of the granite stones found lying about in the take; they are not put together with mortar, but are loosely built up one stone on another, and the wind blows through the interstices. More nasty accidents would happen over these walls, were it not that the moor turf is spongy and boggy, so that when a man is thrown he is lightly received.

Concerning this Bellever week there exists a song—

"Bellever week is the bravest week
Of fifty-two in the year.
'Tis one to tweak a teetotaller's beak,
And to make a Methody swear.
We leave our troubles and toils behind,
Forget if we've got gray hair—
A parcel of boys, all frolic and noise,
Bidding begone dull care.
Bellever week is the bravest, &c.

There's never a run so brimming with fun,
Nor a pastime that may compare,
For master or horse, o'er heather and gorse,

139

As hunting a Dartmoor hare.
Though sure of a stogg to the girths in a bog,
Or a turn up of heels at a wall,
Yet never a jot of damage was got
By a flounder there, or a fall.
Bellever week, &c.

There's nowhere a puss deserving a cuss
For running as on the moor.
In Bellever week the harriers speak
As they never spoke before.
The Saracen's Head is full as an egg,
And every farm and cot.
The jolliest set together are met
In the out and out jolliest spot.
Bellever week, &c.

Nowhere else does a joke such laughter provoke,
Or a tale so hearty a roar,
Or a song that is sung with stentorian lung,
More certain of an encore!
When Bellever week returns again,
My wife—let her storm and sneer;
If not tucked into bed with a stone at my head,
By Ginger!—I will be there.
Bellever week, &c."

How full life is of coincidences! We are always encountering and wondering at them. To some the coincidences that we know to be true seem incredible. Here is one.

The master of a very notable pack of foxhounds died. He had been master for something like thirty years; his father was master before him, and his son is master after him. A man of intense love of the sport. In the dining-room hang the portraits of three generations, all in pink. He died and was buried amidst universal sorrow. Of course the pack did not go out that week. The first meet after the funeral was at a distance of very many miles. The fox was started, and ran, straight as an arrow, towards the residence of the late master, ran through the park, pursued by the hounds, ran across the garden to the churchyard, ran to the vault, and took refuge against the iron door that closed it, and concealed the coffin of the dead M.F.H. And there, against his vault door, the fox was killed, and the yelping, bounding, barking pack careered within a few feet of his coffin.

This story I believe to be perfectly true. It was a coincidence, and a singular one.

Till the end of the seventeenth century fox-hunting can scarcely be said to have existed as a sport in England, the stag, the buck, and the hare taking the precedence with our forefathers as objects of the chase, which in a still earlier period had included the wolf and the boar. And yet I have over my hall fireplace, in the carved oak chimney-piece, a representation of a fox-hunt that certainly belongs to the reign of Elizabeth. The hunters are armed with pitchforks, or something much like them; one is holding back a greyhound by a leash; another is winding a horn. There are ten dogs in the pack, long-eared beagles or dachshunds, it is hard to say what. The fox has eaten one goose all but the head and wings, and has killed a second, and is taking refuge in a pinery among the pine-apples.

Our deer-parks about the great mansions are the remnants of deer-parks or chases that were originally found about the manor-houses in most places. They were not always very extensive, very often were only small paddocks where the deer were kept; and one was let run occasionally for a grand chase. These old paddocks with the ruined walls about them, or without, when they were surrounded by palings, that have long ago rotted away, still go by the name of the Chase, and so remind us of the sports of our forefathers.

James I. was an enthusiastic sportsman. Although in his various kennels he had little short of two hundred couple of hounds, and the cost of their maintenance was a serious draught upon his privy purse, yet he never seemed satisfied that he had enough, so long as he heard of any good hound in the possession of a subject. Among the State Papers is an amusing letter relative to a piece of ill-luck that befell a favourite dog. "The king is at Tibbalds, and the queen gone or going to him. At this last meeting, being at Tibbalds, which was about a fortnight since, the queen, shooting at a deer with her crossbow, mistook her mark, and killed Jewell, the king's most special and principal hound, at which he stormed exceeding awhile, swearing many and great oaths. None would undertake to break unto him the news, so they were fain to send Archie the fool on the errand. But after he knew who did it, he was soon pacified, and with much kindness wished her not to be troubled with it, for he should love her never the worse, and the next day sent her a jewell worth £2000, 'as a legacy from his dead dog.' Love and kindness increase daily between them, and it is thought they were never on better terms."

Our early hunting songs all concern the stag. One of the very "ancientest ditties" we have is, The Hunt is upp—

"The hunt is up, the hunt is up,
And it is well-nigh day;
And Harry our king is gone hunting,
To bring his deer to bay."

A very pretty song it is of the reign of bluff Hal, but the earliest song relating to a fox that I know is that of To-morrow the Fox will come to Town, of the same period, and in that there is no mention of reynard as an object of sport. His thievish qualities are recorded, that is all.

"To-morrow the fox will come to town,
Keep, keep, keep, keep!
To-morrow the fox will come to town,
O keep you all well there.
I must desire you neighbours all,
To hallo the fox out of the hall,
And cry as loud as you can call,
Whoop, whoop, whoop, whoop!
And cry as loud as you can call,
O keep you all well there."

In the porch of Lewanick church, in Cornwall, the piece of freestone that supports the seat on which the gaffers sat before and after church is sculptured with a hare-hunt. The date is about the fifteenth century. In the popular mind the hare-hunt, for the reason already given, that it allows of better sport for the footers, is a favourite subject of song rather than the fox-hunt, the delights of which are sung by huntsmen more than by the peasants. It is curious how the reminiscence of famous runs lingers on among the people. There is a great song that used to be sung at all hunting dinners in Devon relative to the achievements of one Arscott of Tetcott, who is supposed still to hunt the country in spirit with a ghostly pack—

"When the tempest is howling his horn you may hear,
And the bay of his hounds in their headlong career;
For Arscott of Tetcott loves hunting so well,
That he breaks for the pastime from heaven—or hell."

CHAPTER XIV

THE COUNTY TOWN

DOES the reader know one of the most fascinating books of a most fascinating of our old writers, Belford Regis, by Miss Mary Russell Mitford? If not, and he or she desires to be carried back on the broad, sweeping, somewhat sad-coloured wings of fancy to the past, to a time before railways, then let Belford Regis be procured, and read, and smiled, and perhaps a little sighed over. As in Our Village the authoress sketched the country, so in Belford Regis did she sketch the little county town at the beginning of the present century.

"About three miles to the north of our village stands the good town of Belford Regis. The approach to it, straight as a dart, runs along a wide and populous turnpike road, all alive with carts and coaches, waggons and phaetons, horse-people and foot-people, sweeping rapidly or creeping lazily up and down the gentle undulations with which the surface of the country is varied; and the borders, checkered by patches of common, rich with hedgerow timber, and sprinkled with cottages, and, I grieve to say, with that cottage pest, the beer-house,—and here and there enlivened by dwellings of more pretension and gentility,—become more thickly inhabited as we draw nearer the metropolis of the county, to say nothing of the three cottages all in a row, with two small houses attached, which a board affixed to one of them informs the passer-by is Two-mile Cross; or of these opposite neighbours, the wheelwrights and the blacksmiths, about half a mile further; or the little farm close by the pound; or the series of buildings called the Long Row, terminating at the end next the road with an old-fashioned and most picturesque public-house, with painted roofs, and benches at the door and round the large elm before it—benches which are generally filled by thirsty wayfarers and waggoners watering their horses, and partaking of a more generous liquor themselves.

"Leaving these objects undescribed, no sooner do we get within a mile of the town, than our approach is indicated by successive market-gardens on either side, crowned, as we ascend the long hill on which the turnpike-gate stands, by an extensive nursery-ground, gay with long beds of flowers, with trellised walks covered with creepers, with whole acres of flowering shrubs, and ranges of green-houses, the glass glittering in the southern sun. Then the turnpike gate, with its civil keeper, then another public-house, then the clear bright pond on the top of the hill, and then the rows of small tenements, with here and there a more ambitious single cottage standing in its own pretty garden, which forms the usual gradation from the country to the town.

"About this point, where one road, skirting the great pond and edged by small houses, diverges from the great southern entrance, and where two streets, meeting or parting, lead by separate ways down the steep hill to the centre of the town, stands a handsome mansion, surrounded by orchards and pleasure-grounds, across which is perhaps to be seen the very best view of Belford, with its long ranges of modern buildings in the outskirts, mingled with picturesque old streets, the venerable towers of St. Stephen's and St. Nicholas', the light and tapering spire of St. John's, the huge monastic ruins of the abbey, the massive walls of the county gaol, the great river winding along like a thread of silver, trees and gardens mingling amongst all, and the whole landscape environed and lightened by the drooping elms of the foreground, adding an illusive beauty to the picture by breaking the too formal outline, and veiling just exactly those parts which most require concealment.

"Nobody can look at Belford from this point without feeling that it is a very English and very charming scene, and the impression does not diminish on farther acquaintance. We see at once the history of the place, that it is an antique borough town, which has recently been extended to nearly double its former size; so that it unites in no common degree the old romantic, irregular structures in which our ancestors delighted, with the handsome and uniform buildings which are the fashion now-a-days. I suppose that people are right in their taste, and that the modern houses are pleasantest to live in, but, beyond all question, those antique streets are the prettiest to look at. The occasional blending too is good. Witness the striking piece of street scenery which was once accidentally forced upon my attention as I took shelter from a shower of rain in a shop about ten doors up the right-hand side of Friar Street—the old vicarage-house of St. Nicholas embowered in greens, the lofty town-hall, and the handsome modern house of my friend Mr. Beauchamp, the fine church tower of St. Nicholas, the picturesque piazza underneath, the jutting corner of Friar Street, the old irregular shops in the market-place, and the trees of the Forbury just peeping between, with all their varieties of light and shadow. I went to the door to see if the shower was over, was caught by its beauty, and stood looking at it in the sunshine long after the rain had ceased."

144

I make no apology for this long extract. Miss Mitford is not much read now, and those who read her are always glad to re-read a passage from her fresh and graphic pen.

That there may be more picturesqueness in an old German, Italian, and French town may be admitted, but it is of a more salient, obtrusive character than that which exists in our old county towns. The continental architects aimed at bold effects. I do not say that they were wrong. They achieved great success. Our architects built what was wanted, in a quiet, undemonstrative manner, and left effect to chance, and chance gave what they did not seek. The charms of an old English county town do not force themselves on our notice, are missed altogether by the hasty visitor; they have to be found out, they come by surprises, they depend on certain lights and plays of shadow, on the bursting into leaf of certain trees, on the setting up of certain hucksters' stalls. That a great deal of their picturesqueness is passing away is, alas! only too true. The tradesmen want huge window spaces for the display of their goods, so away is knocked the quaint old frontage of the house, and is replaced by something that can be sustained on iron supports between wide sheets of plate-glass. The suburbs are being made hideous with rows of model cottages, all precisely alike, roofed with blue slate. Nevertheless a great deal remains, and it is fortunately now something like a fashion to give us Queen Anne (so-called) gables in the streets, which at all events afford a pretty broken sky-line, and a play of light and shade on the frontage.

Then how different are the outskirts of a foreign town to an English country town. In Italy there are miles of lanes between high stone walls, over which indeed lemons show their glorious fruit and blaze in the sun; nevertheless, the sorry fact remains, that for as far as one cares to walk there is no prospect save by favour through a gate.

At Florence, for instance, it is wall, wall, on the right hand and on the left, all the way to Fiesole; and to the south, beyond S. Miniato, up and down the hills, wall, wall, on the right hand and on the left. At Genoa the city is engirded with hills, indeed the town lies in a crater, broken down to the west to the sea. Climb near two thousand feet to the encircling fortresses, and you go between wall, wall, all the way. Escape along the sea to Sampierdarema on one side, on the other to St. Fruttuoso, and it is a way between wall and house, house and wall. And a French town, or a German town, or a Belgian town, starts up suddenly out of bare fields, without trees, without hedges, with a suburb of tall, hideous, stuccoed, badly-built houses, all precisely alike and equally ugly. There are no cottages.

145

Come back to England, and at once you discover that the cottage is that which gives charm to the approach of a town, it is the moss, the lichen that adheres to the wall, a softening, beautiful feature in itself. Then there are our hedges and hedgerow trees, and how different from the stiff avenues of poplar, and the boulevards of set planes, exactly ten paces apart.

Every foreign city was fortified, and outside the fortifications the glacis had to be kept clear of trees and buildings, so as not to give cover to the enemy. This fact has influenced the approach to all continental towns, they are not led up to as in England; and the poor are lodged differently—they occupy big houses, which they delight in making untidy, and exposing the dishevelled condition of their dwellings to every passer-by. The very lanes between walls are untidy—every possible scrap of refuse collects in them, the stray feathers of fowls that have been plucked throughout the year eddy there, old rags—discarded only when dropping off—rot there, scraps of tin canister are kicked about there, old boots get sodden there. But there is always an effort after tidiness about English cottages; and somehow the approaches to our towns are not offensive to eye and nose, but quite the reverse; the pretty cottages, their well-cared-for gardens, the villas with bosquets of seringa and lilac, combine in making the approach full of studies for the painter—reposeful pictures of general comfort and happiness.

In a foreign town the palace jostles with the gaunt house in which the poor herd. In England there are no palaces in our country towns, but there are excellent middle-class mansions, the Queen Anne red brick tall house, with stone quoins, where lives the substantial solicitor, who makes the wills and draws up the leases for all the squires of the neighbourhood, who is clerk of the Petty Sessions, and is consulted by every one more as a confidential friend than as a professional man. There is the prim house, with exactly as many windows on one side of the door as on the other, and a round-headed window over it, where three old ladies keep a school for girls. There is the many-gabled house inhabited by the late rector's widow. There is the quaint slated house with its bow-windows, within rich with beautiful plaster work and carved wood, supposed to be by Grinling Gibbons. It has a garden in terraces descending to the river, with vases on the balustrade of the terraces full of scarlet geraniums. Then there comes the modern county bank of cut stone, and of inconceivable incongruity and ugliness; then an old inn frequented by the Tory squires in past days. There is the old grammar school with its pedimented door and ivy creeping over the red-brick walls, fought with every year, and forced back from

146

overrunning the windows, as it has overrun the walls. There is the doctor's house, with a portico supported by slim Corinthian pillars, and with a lead above, on which the doctor's wife sets out her flowers, that make a blaze of colour up and down the street. There is the stuccoed wine merchant's house—always painted drab every third year—that has red blinds, through which the lamps at night diffuse a ruby glow into the street. There is that long wall with an elaborately wrought iron gate, with link extinguishers to the side posts, and a small but overgrown garden of shrubs, behind which lurks a thatched cottage where lives a widow—Lady This or That, the mother of the present baronet who resides three miles off at the park. There is the rectory, with its back to the street, and windows so low that the passers-by can see in—or could till they were furnished with twisted cane screens. But then the other side of the parsonage looks into the most charming of gardens, on what was the city wall, whence a glorious view is obtained. But the space would fail me were I to describe, or merely indicate, the various houses of people, some professional, some retired gentry, some retired tradespeople, in a country town, all speaking of comfort, ease, and peace.

Thus wrote Horace Walpole in 1741, on his return to England from Italy—"The country-town (and you will believe me, who you know am not prejudiced) delights me; the populousness, the ease, the gaiety, the well-dressed everybody amaze me. Canterbury—which on my setting out I thought deplorable—is a paradise to Modena, Reggio, Parma, etc. I had before discovered that there was nowhere but in England the distinction of middling people; I perceive now that there is peculiar to us middling houses;—how snug they are!"

How sleepy the dear old country town is on all days of the week save market-day. The shopkeepers do not think it necessary to remain behind their counters, but run across the street or the square to have a chat with each other, and should a purchaser appear, it interrupts a gossip where two or three tradesmen are together; or if the purchaser goes into a deserted shop, he has to wait whilst the owner is fetched from some neighbour's, whither he has gone to discuss the new scheme for water supply, or the bad quality of the gas. Every squire's carriage, every parson's trap of the neighbourhood is known to every one in the town; and should one come in on a day that is not market-day, the reason of its appearance is a subject of much conjecture and discussion.

But how the town wakes up on market-day; how all the tradesmen recover from somnolence, and are nimble on their feet, and full of promises to get this bit of ironmongery attended to at once, such lamp-chimneys fitted, to write to London to order such a lace or such a silk matched—out of stock only yesterday, and to get this watch cleaned, or to reset a stone in that ring, or to alter the stuffing of such a lady's saddle that galls, or to provide so many pounds of cake for a school-treat; and the milliner is hard at work all day fitting gowns, or trying on hats; and the hairdresser's fingers are never resting from snip, snip, snip, and the boy from working the treadmill that sets the rotary-brush in motion; and the ostler is engaged in taking his shillings; and the fishmonger in serving up his baskets of soles and mackerel; and the nursery-gardener in making up bouquets; and the oil-man in filling cans with benzoline, which have to go back under the coachman's feet, as has also a crate with plates from the crockery-shop—that tiresome kitchen-maid does bang the plates about so that she has not left one unsnipped; and the photographer is occupied the whole day setting heads into an apparatus for holding them steady, and pulling down or drawing up blinds; and the dentist is also engaged in relieving persons with swollen cheeks; and in the workhouse congregate the Board of Guardians, and talk over the merits of such and such a case, and the allowance to be made per week.

There are notices about on all the walls that amateur theatricals will be given in the new Town Hall in behalf of the local Hunt; and the neighbours are bringing in their fox's brushes and masks wherewith to decorate the proscenium and the walls of the hall. The poor old Assembly Room, something like a Grecian temple, but copied—and badly copied—in stucco, is now given up to a dealer in antiquities, second-hand furniture, and old china. That Assembly Room in which our grandmothers danced is now piled up with beds, large oil-paintings, chiffoniers, fire-irons and fenders, staircase clocks, and an endless amount of rubbish for which no one, one would suppose, could be found to be purchaser. The assembly balls, the hunt balls, the bachelors' balls, the concerts, and, as we have seen, the dramatical entertainments, now take place in the new Town Hall.

The old county town is thriving. It is a place to which all the neighbourhood gravitates. There is now a setting of the tide into towns, and ebb in the country places. Servants will not go to the country. Meat, dairy produce, fowls, are as dear in the country as in the towns. In the towns it is not necessary to keep a pony carriage; in the towns there is escape from those village parasites who fall on and eat up those who settle in the country; and in the towns there is more going on. In the towns educational advantages are to be had which are lacking in the country. So, not only do old ladies go to towns, but also families fairly well off; and the country is becoming deserted. Small, pretty houses do not let well there; great houses not at all. So the country towns are eating up the country.

"Clean, airy, and affluent; well paved, well lighted, well watched; abounding in wide and spacious streets, filled with excellent shops and handsome houses;—such is the outward appearance, the bodily form, of our market town," says Miss Mitford concerning Belford; and the description applies to every other county town in England. As for the vital-spark, the life-blood that glows and circulates through the dead mass of mortar and masonry, that I have neither space to describe, nor would one description apply to every other.

www.ingramcontent.com/pod-product-compliance
Lightning Source LLC
Chambersburg PA
CBHW011512170626
46810CB00009B/3338